Lights, Camera, DISASTER!

The Macdonald Hall Series:

This Can't Be Happening at Macdonald Hall!

Go Jump in the Pool

Beware The Fish!

The Wizzle War

The Zucchini Warriors

Lights, Camera, Disaster!

The Joke's on Us

GORDON KORMAN

Lights, Camera, DISASTER!

Previous title: *Macdonald Hall Goes Hollywood*

Cover by Paul Perreault

Scholastic Canada Ltd.
Toronto New York London Auckland Sydney
Mexico City New Delhi Hong Kong Buenos Aires

Scholastic Canada Ltd.
604 King Street West, Toronto, Ontario M5V 1E1, Canada
Scholastic Inc.
557 Broadway, New York, NY 10012, USA
Scholastic Australia Pty Limited
PO Box 579, Gosford, NSW 2250, Australia
Scholastic New Zealand Limited
Private Bag 94407, Botany, Manukau 2163, New Zealand
Scholastic Children's Books
Euston House, 24 Eversholt Street, London NW1 1DB, UK

www.scholastic.ca

Library and Archives Canada Cataloguing in Publication
Korman, Gordon
[Macdonald Hall goes Hollywood]
Lights, camera, disaster! / Gordon Korman.
(Macdonald Hall series)
Originally published under title: Macdonald Hall goes Hollywood.
Issued also in electronic format.
ISBN 978-1-4431-2497-3
I. Title. II. Title: Macdonald Hall goes Hollywood.
III. Series: Korman, Gordon. MacDonald Hall series.
PS8571.O78M33 2013   jC813'.54   C2012-907846-8

6 5 4 3 2   Printed in Canada 121   18 19 20 21 22

MIX
Paper from
responsible sources
FSC
www.fsc.org   FSC® C004071

Contents

Chapter 1

Macdonald Hollywood

Movie people swarmed all around Macdonald Hall. From the caravan of trucks and trailers that formed a small village in the easternmost corner of the tree-lined campus, they scrambled like worker ants, anxious to capture every second of sunlight for this first day of shooting.

The trappings of Hollywood were everywhere. Cameras were being mounted on large motorized dollies. Microphones dangled from long booms. Enormous portable reflecting walls were being assembled in a semicircle as technicians took light meter readings. Sound engineers checked background noise. In the makeup trailer, powder-puffs and blush applicators worked furiously and hair dryers screamed. Vehicles, equipment boxes, jackets, even baseball caps were festooned with stickers and buttons advertising the movie. They blazoned: *ACADEMY BLUES, starring Jordie Jones.*

On the main flagpole outside the Faculty Building, the red Maple Leaf of Canada was respectfully lowered and replaced by the Stars and Stripes of the United States of America. The director himself, Seth Dinkman, marched purposefully up to the brass plaque on the ivy-covered stone wall that proclaimed this venerable old institution to be Macdonald Hall. From a plastic bag he produced an identical plaque and snapped it directly over the existing one. It now read: *Georgetown Academy, est. 1851.*

One camera began filming ahead of all the rest, and it did not belong to Dinkman's Hollywood film crew. It was a video recorder operated by Mark Davies.

"This is perfect!" he said, not taking his eye from the viewfinder. "I can start with a long shot of the people setting up."

Pete Anderson scowled at him. "I don't think it's fair that you get out of a whole term of English just to make a dumb movie about a bunch of guys making a dumb movie."

"I'm not getting out of anything," Mark explained patiently. "I'm doing a documentary on the making of *Academy Blues.* I'll be working harder than any of you guys."

Boots O'Neal shifted his position on the grass. "I can't believe this is happening here. Being the set for a movie doesn't seem like Macdonald Hall's style. I figured The Fish would just give them some big lecture about how movie-making would interfere with our studies."

"Actually, Mr. Sturgeon's the most excited guy in the place," grinned Larry Wilson. Larry was the office messenger and usually knew more about what was going on than most of the staff. "He thinks shooting a film here will be educational. Some of us might get to be in it, too. They need lots of extras for crowd scenes."

For the first time in an hour, Mark put down the camera and sat on the grass. "Hey, where's Bruno? I'm surprised he wasn't the first guy out here."

Boots snorted. "It's too early. Bruno wouldn't get up before nine if they were filming the parting of the Red Sea in our toilet bowl."

"He'll show up," said Larry confidently. "The only thing Bruno ever misses around here is class."

As if on cue, the main entrance of Dormitory 3 swung wide, and out into the bright spring sunshine stepped Bruno Walton, a splendid figure. His normally unruly dark hair was greased back to a smooth high polish, and his face was partially obscured by gigantic mirrored sunglasses. He wore a bright red crushed-velvet smoking jacket, loosely tied at the waist. Around his neck lay the elegant folds of a white silk ascot.

"Who's that guy?" asked Pete.

Groaning, Boots got to his feet. "I'm not sure, but I think it's my roommate. Hey, Bruno — what's with the monkey suit?"

Flashing a toothy grin, Bruno jogged over, careful to keep the ascot from unravelling. "That good, eh? I rented it in town. Eight bucks." He surveyed his friends with disapproval. "You guys are so stupid. This place is crawling with directors, producers, cameramen and talent scouts, and here you are, sitting around looking like a bunch of kids. This could be the greatest day of our lives!"

"That's it! I knew it!" Boots exploded. "You think you're going to be a star, don't you?"

"People get discovered every day," lectured Bruno. "But first they have to notice you."

"They're going to notice you, all right," said Boots. "They're going to say, 'Who's the greaseball in the red pyjamas?'

Besides, if they needed a star, they wouldn't have hired Jordie Jones."

"Oh, him." Bruno shrugged. "Of course I don't expect to be the main character. I figure I'll start off with a couple of crowd scenes and really steal the show. Then they'd be nuts not to give me a great part."

"Well, we already *know* who's nuts," said Boots sarcastically.

"There aren't any parts up for grabs," Larry protested. "They just want students to be in the background."

"They *think* that's all they want," said Bruno brightly. "They're making a movie about boarding school. What do a bunch of Hollywood guys know about it? Nothing. They *need* us. Hey, Mark, get a shot of a typical Macdonald Hall student prepared for his film debut."

"I hope you don't mean you," said Mark.

"Bruno — " began Boots carefully. "Remember the assembly on Friday? Remember what The Fish was saying?"

"He said this was going to be a great learning experience for us," said Bruno.

"He also said no bugging the movie guys!"

"Who's bugging?" Bruno was the picture of injured innocence. "We're helping."

"*We're* not doing anything," Boots insisted. "If you want to get in big trouble and make an idiot of yourself as usual, you'd better know that you're alone this time. I'm going to keep my nose clean and do exactly what The Fish said. If I wind up in a crowd scene and get to be in the movie, that's great. If I don't, that's okay, too. Right, guys?"

"Right," chorused Larry, Mark and Pete.

Bruno's smile didn't waver. "I have no hard feelings. Even though you're being morons now, I'm still going to put in a good word for you when I'm tight with the director."

By seven o'clock everything was ready, and Dinkman checked the angle of the last camera. Then, satisfied, he picked up a small old-fashioned school bell and rang it. Everyone stood, expectantly facing the furthest trailer, which was set off from the others for extra privacy. It was actually a luxury camper with a large gold star painted on the door. The door opened a crack, and out peered one of the most famous faces in the world.

An enormous cheer rocked the countryside. Across the road from Macdonald Hall, the renowned Miss Scrimmage's Finishing School for Young Ladies erupted into life. Faces jammed every window, and a line of girls five deep appeared on the roof. Out the front door burst the school's marching band, followed by an honour guard carrying field hockey sticks like rifles. From Miss Scrimmage's second floor balcony a gigantic banner unfurled. It read:

WE ♥ U, JORDIE JONES

Signs on bedsheets, reading WELCOME, JORDIE, framed in all manner of hearts and flowers, fluttered everywhere.

The young blond movie star stepped out onto the lawn and waved, and the girls went berserk for ten minutes.

Bruno looked from the star to the chaos at Miss Scrimmage's. "*Un*-believable!" he said in disgust. He had to shout just to be heard over the ruckus.

"I think they've got a few Jordie Jones fans across the road," said Boots dryly.

Bruno snorted. "Jordie Jones — big deal. I've seen him in that TV series he made when he was three — *Cutesy Newbar*. What a joke! All he did was drool and have his diaper fall down! That's not acting! That's hanging a moon!"

Larry goggled. "*He* was Cutesy Newbar?"

"Sure," said Bruno. "You didn't recognize him with his pants on. If he'd *backed* out of that trailer with his diaper around his knees, you'd have said, 'Hey, look — Cutesy Newbar.'"

Boots smiled sardonically. "Well, he's a big star, and you're not."

"Not today," amended Bruno.

"Shhh!" The camera was back in Mark's hand. "They're getting started!"

Director Dinkman raised an electric megaphone to his lips. "Okay, sports fans, listen up. We're going to start with everybody's favourite — connecting shots of Jordie walking around the campus." There were loud groans from the crew. *"Yeah, I know. It's boring. But we'll need a lot of this footage when we're putting the picture together. So let's get it over with. We'll want some kids in the background. You, you, you — "* he began to point at random to the Macdonald Hall boys grouped behind the sawhorses that partitioned off the filming area, *" — you and you. Props, get these guys some stuff."*

Whooping and cheering, the five chosen extras scampered over to where two property men were handing out armloads of books, backpacks, a baseball and two gloves.

"Wait a second," said Bruno in consternation. "You mean

that's it? Five lousy guys?" He put up his hand and called over to the director, "Uh, sir — sir — "

Dinkman looked up, spotted Bruno and stared. "Can I do something for you, pal?"

Bruno cleared his throat carefully. "Well — uh — I don't like to complain, but the way you picked those guys — you know — 'you, you, you, you and you' — seems kind of careless."

Dinkman laughed. "Actually, it was very scientific. I said to myself, 'Who looks like a normal kid, and who looks like a Christmas cracker?'" He turned back to his cameraman.

"Uh, sir," Bruno persisted. "Sir — "

"Shhh!" hissed Boots. "Cut it out!"

Dinkman looked up, frowning slightly. "I'm a little busy," he said, still pleasantly.

"Well, it's just that I think it would be a lot more fair — " began Bruno.

The director was no longer patient. "Kid, life isn't fair. The movie business isn't fair. The guy who sold you that jacket *really* isn't fair. And it's not fair to the producers, who are footing the bill at almost $14,000 an hour, for me to be standing here arguing with you, because it's costing over two hundred bucks a minute."

As Bruno stood boiling, the director deployed his extras and called, "Action!" The cameras followed Jordie Jones as he made his way across the lawn. With every step of his famous feet, the volume from Miss Scrimmage's seemed to quadruple.

Boots put a sympathetic arm around his roommate's velvet shoulders. "Forget it, Bruno. Let's go get some breakfast."

Bruno didn't seem to hear. "That guy doesn't know what he's doing," he said through clenched teeth. "He's just going to have to learn the hard way. Look who he's got out there throwing a baseball — Sidney Rampulsky, the world champion klutz! He had to quit Little League because he kept tripping over centre field!"

They watched Sidney and Calvin Fihzgart toss a hardball back and forth as the star meandered across the lawn and the cameras rolled. But when Calvin's toss went a little high, Sidney had to scramble back for it. On the recovery and return he slipped on the grass, and the throw went wild. It sizzled over Jordie Jones's shoulder, missing his ear by barely a centimetre, and slammed into one of the reflecting walls, knocking it off balance. It toppled into the next one, which in turn knocked over a third, and soon they all went down like dominoes. The Macdonald Hall boys broke into appreciative applause.

"No-o-o-o!" From the sidelines, a streak of white barrelled across the lawn, hurdling equipment and technicians alike. In front of Jordie Jones, the whirlwind stopped and resolved itself into a short chubby man dressed entirely in glaring white California sports clothes.

"J.J., are you all right? Talk to me!" The waving of his arms was creating a breeze that riffled the jet-black toupee perched on the top of his head like a small animal staking out its territory. His eyes, through thick glasses, were wild.

The young star shrugged. "I'm fine, Goose. It didn't even touch me."

"Cut! *Cut!*" Dinkman glared at the little man in white. "Get off my set, you lunatic!"

Goose Golden bristled. "As Jordie's personal manager, I formally protest this unnecessary risk to his well-being!"

Dinkman looked disgusted. "It was a baseball, not a hand grenade. Beat it, Goose, before your face breaks the cameras."

Golden put a protective arm around Jordie. "My client refuses to work until safety conditions have improved on this set."

The director reddened. "You're the most annoying idiot in Hollywood! You haven't changed since you represented Waldo the Waltzing Alley Cat!"

"I still don't think catnip breaks are unreasonable," the manager said righteously. He reached into his white warm-up jacket and produced a thick legal document. "Now, if you'll refer to the 'Dangers to Person' clause of J.J.'s contract, page 31, subsection 19C, paragraph (ii) — "

Dinkman sighed heavily and turned to Sidney. "Sorry, kid. You're history." Golden looked triumphant. "Okay, we need another ballplayer. You." His finger was pointing at Bruno and Boots. Bruno jumped forward eagerly. "No, not you, Casanova. The blond kid beside you."

"Aw, come on!" cried Bruno in exasperation. Tossing a sideways grin over his shoulder, Boots took over Sidney's glove. By this time, the reflecting walls were back in place, and the filming began again. Sidney jogged over to Bruno. "I washed out," he said sadly.

But Bruno was already sauntering casually past the sawhorses, edging ever closer to camera range. "Pssst! Bruno!" This from Boots between catches. "Get out of here!"

Bruno grinned blissfully and continued his stroll. An excited murmur passed through the ranks of the Macdonald Hall students.

"Hey, check out Bruno!" exclaimed Larry. "He's putting himself in the movie!"

His hands clasped behind his back, Bruno promenaded like a retired millionaire surveying his estate. By this time, all the boys had noticed him and were watching in fascination. He walked right up to Jordie Jones, murmured, "Hey, how ya doin'?" and kept on going.

"Cut! *Cut!*" Seth Dinkman's face was approaching the colour of Bruno's jacket. "Kid — " he began.

An all-too-familiar voice interrupted. "Walton," it said, "perhaps you can spare me a minute of your valuable time."

Everyone wheeled. William R. Sturgeon, alias The Fish, Headmaster of Macdonald Hall, stood behind the sawhorses, arms folded.

Boots put his hand over his eyes.

"Good morning, Mr. Sturgeon," said Bruno brightly. "We've started *Academy Blues*. I'm a typical student walking across the campus."

"And that, no doubt, is the new school uniform," said the Headmaster. He turned to Dinkman. "I trust you can shoot around him for the next little while?"

"Please," said the director gratefully.

"Come along, Walton," said Mr. Sturgeon, "and we shall discuss last Friday's assembly, and how I rarely speak just to hear the sound of my own voice."

Reluctantly Bruno trailed off after the Headmaster. Soon he was seated on the hard wooden bench in the main office of the

Faculty Building, facing Mr. Sturgeon across his massive oak desk.

"Now, Walton, bearing in mind that I know you were not selected as an extra for that scene, I require an explanation as to why you were right in the thick of the action."

"Well, sir," said Bruno, "you know how it is."

"Enlighten me."

"They just needed a bunch of guys goofing around," Bruno explained, a little shamefaced. "They picked five, and I figured what's the difference between six and five? I didn't think they'd even notice me."

Mr. Sturgeon's thin lips twitched, but the smile never quite surfaced. "What disturbs me is that my rules were disobeyed — on the very first day, in the very first scene, before breakfast! That must be some sort of record, Walton, even for you."

Bruno studied the carpet. "I'm sorry, sir."

The Headmaster sat back in his padded chair. "When I recommended to our Board that it would be good experience for the boys of Macdonald Hall to host a motion picture crew, my only reservation was that our students might not be mature enough to realize that there would be a time and a place for their participation. Your time and place was not today. You will wait until that time comes. And if that time never comes, you will take it like a man. Do I make myself clear?"

"Yes, sir."

"Good. However, it is necessary that you be punished." He looked Bruno over from head to toe. "Actually, the person who truly merits punishment is your tailor. But as *he* is not a registered student of Macdonald Hall, *you* will pick up litter on the campus every afternoon for one week. Dismissed."

As Bruno scampered off, Mr. Sturgeon heaved a great sigh, unable to shake the feeling that he had left something unsaid. He glanced out the window. Yes, there was Walton, sprinting at top speed, not for the dining hall for breakfast, not for Dormitory 3 to change his clothes, but straight back to the east lawn and the movie set.

* * *

An hour after lights-out that night, Bruno and Boots crouched in the window of room 306 in Dormitory 3, scanning the deserted campus.

Boots stuck his head and shoulders out the window and looked over toward the Housemaster's room.

"Fudge's light is still on," he whispered.

Bruno glanced at his watch in annoyance. "Doesn't he know what time it is? Anybody up this late has no business being a Housemaster. What a lousy example he's setting for us students. Okay, he's got five minutes. Then I'm going, no matter what."

Boots laughed. "You're just looking for someone to keep you company on garbage patrol."

"I hate waiting," growled Bruno. "It's almost as thrilling as making a movie! Do you believe those idiots? Thirteen hours of Cutesy Newbar walking around! And tomorrow the shooting schedule calls for thirteen *more* hours of Cutesy Newbar walking around. I mean, what kind of a movie is this — a training film on walking?"

"You heard Mr. Dinkman," said Boots. "They don't just film

the script scene by scene. They do it out of order and edit it together at the end. They're not even shooting the whole movie here — just the outside stuff. They're doing the interiors in California."

"I think they're just covering up the fact that they're not too bright," grumbled Bruno. "I mean, stupid Cutesy must have changed his clothes twenty times today. And for what? Walking around."

"Mr. Dinkman explained all that," said Boots. "They need to get him in every outfit. That way, when they cut from an inside shot to him walking, he'll be wearing the right stuff. Hey, Fudge's light just went out." Now that the coast was clear, the two boys eased themselves over the sill and stepped outside into the cover of the bushes. Then, silently, they darted past the dormitories, scampered across the highway and scaled the wrought-iron fence surrounding Miss Scrimmage's Finishing School for Young Ladies. "It's amazing to see the place so quiet," observed Boots, gazing up at the darkened windows.

"It's amazing to see the place still standing," said Bruno in disgust, "after the display they put on every time his Royal Cutesiness blew his nose. I'm going to have something to say to Cathy about that." He picked up a handful of pebbles and tossed them at a second-floor window.

A shadowy head appeared. "Come on up."

Boots in the lead, they shinnied up the drainpipe.

"Just don't start chewing them out until we've heard their side of the story," Boots whispered. "I'm sure Cathy and Diane had nothing to do with that teenybopper stuff. They probably don't even like Jordie Jones."

At the window, blonde Diane Grant helped them into the room.

Bruno and Boots stared. The walls were plastered with posters of Jordie Jones movies, with eight-by-ten glossies of the actor himself filling in every available space. Several of the WELCOME, JORDIE signs lay in the corner under a stack of movie magazines that featured the teen idol. Diane wore a Jordie Jones T-shirt and a button featuring three-year-old Jordie's face as Cutesy Newbar.

At that moment, the door opened and Cathy Burton whirled in. "Great news, Diane! Wilma sold us the mug!" She waved a glass coffee cup with Jordie Jones's smiling face, then caught sight of Bruno and Boots. "Oh, fantastic, you're here! What's he like?"

Bruno knew exactly what she was talking about, but he folded his arms in front of him and set his jaw. "What's who like?"

"Jordie, of course!"

"Jordie — Jordie — " mused Bruno. "It doesn't ring a bell."

Cathy exploded. "You walked right by him! You spoke to him! We saw you!"

"Oh," said Bruno in sudden recognition. "You must mean Cutesy Newbar. Well, let me think. It's kind of hard to judge because he had his pants on. But on the whole, all things considered, I would estimate that, on a scale of one to ten, I liked him about negative twelve."

"Why?" wailed Diane. "What did he say to you?"

"*Say?*" repeated Bruno, as though she had suggested the impossible. "Speak to a common peasant? Don't be ridiculous.

He might lose his standing as a conceited jerk."

"To be fair," Boots put in, "you were in the middle of where you weren't supposed to be. They gave out scripts, and I don't remember any part where a guy in a red velvet jacket comes by for a conversation."

"You're just jealous," added Diane.

"Of Cutesy Newbar?" Bruno exploded. "I feel sorry for the guy. How would you like it if, by your third birthday, everybody on earth with a TV set had already had a good look at your *derrière*? Frankly, I don't see how he can show his face in public."

"Cut it out," pleaded Cathy. "We need your help to figure out some way to get to meet him!"

"Wait a second," said Boots in annoyance. "What do we look like — marriage brokers?"

"Oh, please!" Diane wheedled. "Just do this one little favour!"

"Seems like we're doing you a lot of favours this year," Bruno snapped. "How about all those fireworks we're hiding for Miss Scrimmage's golden anniversary celebration?"

"Who can think of a bunch of dumb fireworks when Jordie Jones is right across the road?" squealed Cathy.

"I can," said Boots feelingly. "Especially if The Fish calls a dorm inspection and finds thirty kilos of dynamite under our beds! Or worse, if they go off and blow us to kingdom come!"

"Now you're being paranoid," said Cathy. "See what jealousy does to a person? Look how mad you're getting."

Bruno swung a leg over the windowsill. "This isn't mad at all. This is a friendly disagreement. Mad is when the guy goes home and never comes back again. And if he sees Cutesy Newbar on the way, he gives him a good swift kick in the part that made him so famous." He heaved himself outside and began to descend.

After a shrug at Cathy and Diane that was half reproach and half apology, Boots followed.

Chapter 2

Tap-Dancing Garbage Picker

Wilbur Hackenschleimer, amateur weightlifter, gourmet and Macdonald Hall's largest student, was also on garbage detail. Wilbur was there when Bruno arrived at the caretaker's office to pick up his pointed stick and trash bag.

"Yeah, it was a food rap," Wilbur was saying as the two took to the campus. "The Fish didn't mind me having the toaster oven and the microwave, but he got kind of steamed about the indoor barbecue with rotating spit. He said it violated the dorm fire code."

"Picky, picky," said Bruno sympathetically. "Well, I'm here for exhibiting the kind of creative thought that made this country great."

"Yeah, I heard," said Wilbur. "You snuck into the movie, eh?"

"What movie?" snarled Bruno. "All I see is a conceited snot-nose walking back and forth. Not my idea of an action flick."

"They gave us copies of the shooting script," Wilbur pointed out. "Didn't you read it?"

"I tried to," said Bruno. "It didn't make any sense. It was all about this kid Steve. I mean, who's Steve?"

"Steve's the main character," Wilbur explained patiently. "Jordie Jones plays Steve. His folks send him to Georgetown Academy, and he really hates it — "

"Okay. I got that far," Bruno interrupted. "But then the guy starts flushing all this weird stuff down the toilet, like socks, baseball cards, flowers, a grapefruit — "

"He's trying to mess up the school's plumbing so they'll have to send everybody home."

"That's stupid!" Bruno exploded. "Does The Fish close up Macdonald Hall every time one of the guys clogs up his can? We'd never get to class."

"Yeah, but Steve's going for a total block-up. Only, he forgets about it and starts trying to escape from school. But the teachers always catch him." Wilbur's eyes gleamed. "Here's the best part — meanwhile, the grapefruit has completely jammed up the main sewer pipe."

"Leave it to Cutesy Newbar to co-star with a grapefruit," muttered Bruno in disgust. "I wonder who gets top billing. I vote for the grapefruit."

"The pipe breaks, but they fix it wrong," Wilbur continued, warming to the *Academy Blues* story. "Natural gas leaks into the plumbing and, right at the end of the movie, the whole Faculty Building explodes."

Bruno stared at him. "They're going to blow up the Faculty Building?"

The big boy shrugged. "I think they're using a model."

"Too bad," said Bruno airily. "Actually, the thing that *really* bugs me is that all of Scrimmage's has gone totally gaga over that bonehead Cutesy Newbar, the Rear Admiral."

"He doesn't seem like that bad a guy to me," said Wilbur. "In the interviews I've seen, he wasn't conceited at all."

Bruno made a face. "Just remember that while you ate slop in the dining hall last night, he got into a limo and was whisked off to Toronto for the best meal in town."

"That snob!" said Wilbur angrily. "He could have at least brought us a doggie bag!" He stopped and speared a gum wrapper. "I suppose this is as good a place as any."

"Says you," said Bruno. "I've got a gut feeling that they really need a cleanup over on the east lawn."

* * *

The largest of the film company's trailers was the portable screening room, outfitted like a miniature theatre. Director Dinkman, his cameramen and cinematographer, star Jordie Jones and his personal manager, Goose Golden, were scattered among the trailer's thirty seats, watching the day's footage on a large screen.

Jordie yawned.

Goose leapt to his feet. "The poor child is exhausted! You're running him into the ground! He'll collapse!"

Dinkman looked at his star. "Want to call it a night, Jordie?"

"Of course not. It's only eight o'clock."

"You could go to your trailer and gear down," urged Goose.

"And do what?" asked Jordie. "Play checkers with myself?"

"If you keep up this frenetic pace, you'll get sick!" Goose persisted.

"Hey, Goose," called the director, never taking his eyes from the screen, "maybe you can settle a little bet for us. Dave here says you'd shut up for five minutes if we shoved a projector down your throat, and I say no way. What do you think?" Suddenly he leapt to his feet. "Hey, stop! Run that back!"

The projectionist complied, and all eyes were on Jordie, jogging briskly from one of the dormitories. In the background were two boys tossing around a football, a jogger in sweat pants, three students coming back from class and a lone figure picking up litter with a pointed stick.

It happened in a split second. The garbage picker turned away from his work, looked directly into the camera and waved.

Dinkman slapped himself on the forehead. "Great! Another undiscovered star! Okay, we can cut that part out. Keep rolling."

But a few minutes later, it happened again. Jordie was seated against a tree, doing some homework, when the garbage picker entered the frame, stabbing and stuffing his way in from the left.

"It's him again!" howled Dinkman. In a rage, he turned on his cameramen. "What are you guys — *asleep*? Don't you notice when there's an unauthorized person *on camera*?"

"Aw, boss, we got kids out there. He looks like all the others. We can still use some of this. He isn't doing anything."

But at that moment, the garbage picker interrupted his work to employ his stick as the baton of a great symphony conductor.

Dinkman hit the ceiling. "I'll kill him! I'll find him, and I'll kill him! Fourteen grand an hour, four bucks a second, and we're wasting it shooting *him*!"

"Keep on going," laughed Jordie. "It's just getting interesting."

The scene changed. Now Jordie was walking along with an armload of books, which he dropped, then knelt to pick up. As the shot moved in tight on the star, the garbage picker appeared in the corner of the frame. From the angle of the camera, he looked like a tiny little person perched on the shoulder of a giant.

"I'm not even upset," said Dinkman. "I'm numb. A whole day's shooting down the toilet. How could it be worse?"

No sooner were the words out of his mouth than the tiny figure began to tap dance. Then he pretended to stab himself with his stick and performed an elaborate death scene. And before Jordie stood up again, blocking him out of the picture, he looked into the camera and distinctly mouthed the words, "Hi, Mom."

Jordie Jones was in hysterics, out of his seat, rolling on the carpeted floor.

"Stop that!" cried Goose, horrified. "Don't laugh so hard! You'll get hoarse! You'll get the hiccups! You'll get hepatitis B!"

Jordie only laughed harder. "I've got to meet this guy!"

"Wait a second!" said the director. "I know that face! That's the kid with the red coat!" He snapped his fingers suddenly. "Hey, get the lab on the phone!"

* * *

In the Headmaster's cottage, Mr. Sturgeon placed an eight-by-ten glossy photograph on the kitchen table in front of his wife.

"Mildred, what do you make of this?"

She examined it. "Why, it's Bruno Walton! Doesn't he look handsome!"

"This photograph is being distributed to the entire motion picture crew with instructions to shoot first and ask questions later."

She looked at him quizzically. "Whatever does that mean?"

"It seems that this handsome fellow has been appearing in several scenes in the movie as an uninvited guest star," sighed Mr. Sturgeon. "They're not pleased with him, Mildred. Nor am I." He smiled grimly. "This picture was taken from a frame of film where Walton was performing what was described to me as a rather creditable soft shoe."

She laughed. "I suppose you'll have to punish him."

"That's just the point," the Headmaster said in perplexity. "He was on punishment when he did *this*. The boy is determined to get into *Academy Blues* or die trying. I've extended his punishment and changed it to dishwashing, which will at least keep him indoors. But I really don't see how much further I can go. After all, Walton lives here; the film people are the outsiders."

"Perhaps it wasn't such a good idea to let the movie company on campus," said Mrs. Sturgeon worriedly.

"I wouldn't say that," said the Headmaster. "Look at the Davies boy. He's out there with his video camera every spare second. I've never seen anyone so absorbed. And the boys who are legitimately extras are glowing with enthusiasm. It's just Walton." He shook his head. "Who knows what he's planning even as we speak!"

* * *

Boots O'Neal opened the door of room 306 to find a large globe cedar shrub sitting dead centre on the floor.

"Bruno?" he called. "What's this bush doing here?"

"Hey, Boots," came the reply. "How was class?" Boots looked around nervously. Bruno was nowhere in sight. "Where are you?"

The bush trembled, then rose, and Bruno appeared from its depths. "Hah! It works!"

Boots was still confused. "Are we going to a costume party?"

Bruno laughed diabolically. "Dinkman squealed to The Fish about me yesterday. I bet Cutesy Newbar put him up to it. He can't stand to share the spotlight with anybody else. I don't mind that so much. What gets me is all my scenes are cut out of *Academy Blues*."

Boots laughed. "There probably isn't a tap-dancing garbage picker in the script, you know."

"Well, they'll never spot me in this bush. I'll just blend right into the scenery."

Boots threw himself down on his bed with a groan. "You promised The Fish that you'd stop bugging Mr. Dinkman."

Bruno shrugged. "How can a bush bug anybody? It just sits there."

"*Are* you going to just sit there?" demanded Boots. "Or is this particular bush planning to jump up and recite Shakespeare?"

"Of course not," said Bruno indignantly. "I don't know any Shakespeare."

* * *

Jordie Jones was up early the next morning. While the cast and crew were at breakfast, he had finished his and was sipping a glass of orange juice, leaning against his trailer and watching the dawn break over the deserted campus.

The outline of the ivy-covered Faculty Building became defined, and the three long dormitories appeared in pale gold light and began to cast their shadows over the lawn. The young movie star sighed and wished himself a part of it all.

And then one of the shadows moved.

A large round shape came away from Dormitory 3 and ran stealthily around the side of the building. Intrigued, Jordie jogged over to investigate. But there was nothing there — just the shrubbery that hugged the brick wall.

He frowned in perplexity, positive he had seen something. Finally, with a shrug, he turned to go, taking a big swig of juice. He winced. Jordie hated orange juice, but Goose insisted that he drink lots of it because the vitamin C would fight off scurvy, elephantiasis, paper cuts, etc. Checking that Goose was nowhere around, he tossed the remaining half glass into the bushes and jogged back to his trailer.

A certain globe cedar sputtered and spat.

* * *

"Freeze frame!" barked Seth Dinkman at that night's screening. He got up and stared at the screen intently. "That bush," he said, pointing at a globe cedar, "is not supposed to be there!"

"How's that, boss?" questioned a cameraman.

"Because ten minutes ago it was over by the door!" They all watched closely as the footage continued. When Jordie stood by a window, the bush was there; when he came out the front door, the bush was there; when he appeared around the side of the building, so did the bush.

"Okay," said the director. "*How* did this happen?"

"Well, come on, boss, how are we supposed to know it isn't a real bush?"

Dinkman was raving. "You don't have to be a botanist to know that bushes don't have feet!"

"Look!" cheered Jordie. "They have heads, too! It's that guy!"

"This is ridiculous!" moaned Dinkman. "These private schools are supposed to have so much discipline! Why can't they keep one lousy kid out of my movie?"

* * *

Cathy jumped down from the top of the wrought-iron fence, then reached up and helped Diane.

Diane looked nervous. "What if Jordie Jones doesn't want to meet us at two o'clock in the morning?"

"Well, that's just tough, because the feeling isn't mutual," Cathy replied. "I want to meet him." She grabbed Diane by the arm and dragged her across the highway. Once on Macdonald Hall property, they made straight for the east lawn.

"What do you say to a big star like Jordie Jones?" whined Diane.

"Just because he's famous and adorable and perfect doesn't mean he's any different from the rest of us," Cathy explained. "We introduce ourselves, apologize for the late hour, and he invites us in for a Coke or something. Simple."

"What if he doesn't?"

Cathy was growing impatient. "A perfect gentleman like Jordie Jones would always ask us in. But on the off chance that he forgets, because maybe he was sleeping, we'll drop a subtle hint. You know, like, 'Oh, boy, I'm thirsty.' Look — there's his trailer. Let me do all the talking."

But as they made for the door with the big star on it, there was the sound of running feet, and a ghostly figure interposed itself between the girls and the trailer.

"Sto-o-o-o-op!" bellowed Goose Golden. He was dressed in white pyjamas and a white bathrobe, and brandished a tennis racket like an offensive weapon. His toupee had been slapped on in a hurry and leaned perilously to the left, and he was without his glasses, which gave him a bewildered, squinty look.

"Security!" he howled.

"Shhh!" admonished Cathy. "Do you want to wake everybody up?"

"Yes! *Security!* Someone's trying to kidnap J.J.!"

"We're not kidnappers!" blurted out Diane. "We're fans!"

"We just want to meet him," added Cathy.

"At two o'clock in the morning?" challenged the agent, swinging the racket blindly as though trying to disperse a swarm of bees.

"We're students," Cathy explained reasonably. "When else can we get away?"

The wild motion of the tennis racket stopped, but Goose remained suspicious. "That's exactly what real kidnappers would say! Still, you sound like students." His eyes were tiny slits as he tried to make them out in the moonlight.

But Cathy's attention was focused on the trailer's forward window. A light was on inside, and through the curtains poked the groggy, tousled, famous head of Jordie Jones, investigating the ruckus. She was about to make straight for the window when there were running footsteps, and a gruff voice called, "Hey! What's going on there?"

"Run!" screamed Diane, grabbing her roommate by the arm and attempting to sprint away.

But Cathy stood rooted to the spot, until two burly security men appeared around the back of the trailer and pointed at the girls.

"Hey, you!"

The girls darted for open campus, the guards in hot pursuit. Even in this moment of danger and excitement, Cathy couldn't resist turning around to face the actor in the window. Breathless and running backward at top speed, she screeched, *"Nice to meet you, Jordie!"* heedless of the men bearing down on her.

Confused, Jordie waved. Then, and only then, did Cathy turn her back on the trailer and make her escape.

"They're gaining on us!" quavered Diane between gasps.

"We'll never make it home!" Cathy panted. "Double back and head for Dormitory 3!"

"Dormitory 3?!" repeated Diane. "Bruno and Boots hate us! We'll get fed to Wilbur Hackenschleimer!"

"Well, they'll just have to help anyway! This is an emergency!"

* * *

"There's something going on out there!" exclaimed Boots, peering out the window of room 306.

Bruno rolled over in bed and groaned. "The way I feel right now, I couldn't get up if they were firebombing the dorms. You should try being a bush for a few hours. All that crouching is murder on your back."

Boots hung his head outside. "It's coming from Jordie Jones's trailer!"

"Maybe it's an assassination attempt," muttered Bruno. "Let's just hope the hit men know what they're doing. The nerve of that guy, dumping his stupid orange juice all over me! Like I'm not a person because I'm not the great Rear Admiral Cutesy Newbar!"

"Bruno, most people don't go around checking bushes to make sure there aren't any guys hiding in them. It was probably just an accident."

"He's the big movie star." Bruno snorted. "Everybody hides in bushes in the movies."

Boots stuck his entire body out the window, balancing his torso on the sill. "Sure is a big commotion. Mr. Golden's out there, and Mr. Dinkman, Jordie Jones, a bunch of big guys. And yeah, here comes The Fish. Wonder what it's all about?"

Suddenly, from out of the shadows, a head popped up right in front of Boots. *"Boo!"*

Shocked, Boots lost his balance on the sill and tumbled forward into the bushes.

A laughing Cathy Burton pulled him up by the shoulders. "You should have seen the look on your face. It was classic!"

Boots was white as a sheet. "What are you doing here?" he hissed.

A nervous Diane appeared beside them. "Let's get inside!" she whispered urgently.

They clambered in the window to find Bruno sitting up in bed, a disgusted expression on his face. "What an honour!" he cried sarcastically. "Visiting *us* with His Royal Cutesiness right here on this very campus! The prestige! Gosh, Boots, do we really deserve it?"

"Oh, we just came from Jordie's place," said Cathy airily. "But the security guards chased us away."

Boots snapped to attention. "You mean, all *this*" — he motioned out the window to indicate the chaos on the east lawn — "is — is *you*?"

"This isn't a social call," said Cathy. "We just need someplace to hide out until the heat's off and we can go back home."

Diane sat down heavily on the floor. "I can't believe that you just turned around and introduced yourself to Jordie Jones through two charging gorillas!"

"He waved at me," sighed Cathy. To Bruno and Boots, she added, "While we're here, we may as well pick up those fireworks you've been holding for us."

"But I thought Miss Scrimmage's anniversary wasn't until May," Boots protested.

"Yeah, but Jordie Jones's birthday is this week," said Diane. "We want to throw him a big bash!"

Boots was horrified. "You're giving Jordie Jones Miss Scrimmage's tribute?"

"It's no tribute," countered Cathy. "Miss Scrimmage is afraid of fireworks. We wanted to see if she could climb up the flagpole."

"Still," said Bruno reproachfully, "how would The Fish feel if he hit fifty years teaching without so much as a practical joke from us?"

"Relieved, probably," supplied Boots. "And we'd wash a lot fewer dishes."

"He'd be devastated," Bruno amended. "And even though Miss Scrimmage is kind of wacko, she deserves the same thing."

"Come on, Bruno," said Cathy, pulling a box of Roman candles from under Boots's bed. "You guys can help us get this stuff across the highway."

Just then there was a sharp rapping at the door. "Walton, O'Neal — " came the voice of Mr. Fudge, the Housemaster.

Boots's heart skipped a beat. "Yes, sir?"

Bruno threw a shoe at him. "We're supposed to be asleep!" he hissed. Aloud, he said in the groggiest voice he could muster, "Who is it?"

"Pardon me for rousing you from such a deep sleep, Walton," came the voice of Mr. Sturgeon. "Did your dreams perchance include two of Miss Scrimmage's students hiding out in our dormitory?"

The four exchanged agonized glances. How did Mr. Sturgeon always know exactly what they were doing?

"Uh, why do you ask, sir?" stalled Bruno. Madly, he motioned Cathy and Diane to the open window. They dove for it at exactly the same instant, wedging themselves in the opening. A whispered shouting match ensued, with Boots pushing from behind.

The Headmaster's voice was laced with sarcasm. "Oh, eyewitness accounts of security guards — that sort of thing. Do ask Miss Burton and Miss Grant to be careful. Climbing in and out of buildings can be treacherous."

No sooner were the words out of his mouth than Boots hurled himself bodily against Cathy and Diane. With twin cries of dismay, they were jarred loose, diving over the sill and into the bushes. Wasting no time, they sprinted back to their own campus.

"Oh, yes. One last thing. Both of you are confined to your room after classes for one week's time. Is that clear?"

"Yes, sir!" agreed Bruno, too quickly.

Mr. Sturgeon sensed Bruno's smile. "In your case, Walton, we shall make an exception of the time you are on dishwashing duty. And Walton, since you will be in your room, it follows that you will *not* be on the movie set, either in human form, or as any species of plant life. Goodnight."

Chapter 3

Booby-Trapping the Star

At a secluded table in the dining hall, Bruno Walton was holding court.

"All right, guys, what are we going to do about Cutesy Newbar?"

Larry Wilson looked at him. "Do? The guy's here making a movie. When he's done, he'll leave. What's there to do?"

"We've got to put him in his place. Get him off his high horse. He thinks he can run around like the king of the world, throwing orange juice on everybody — "

"Not everybody," interrupted Boots. "Just you."

"I mean symbolically," amended Bruno. "Besides, he's poisoning their minds at Scrimmage's. We've got the spring dance coming up. How'd you like to spend the evening with a bunch of love-struck Cutesy Newbar zombies? We've got to show this guy who's boss!"

"We already know who's boss," put in Boots. "The Fish is. And we're not allowed out after classes, remember?"

"I've already thought of that. If we go out tonight, that's not after classes. That's before tomorrow's classes."

Pete Anderson looked shocked. "You're right! And to think of all the times I sat in my room, doing confinement on the wrong day!"

Boots ignored him. "Bruno, The Fish is going to kill us if we feed him a line like that."

"The Fish appreciates good logic," said Bruno smugly. "If he's going to punish us, he's going to have to be more specific."

"'You're expelled' is pretty specific."

"If it'll make you feel better," said Bruno kindly, "we can do it after lights-out. That way we won't be violating our confinement, since we aren't allowed out that late, punishment or not."

Wilbur Hackenschleimer peered out from behind an enormous stack of chicken cutlets. "Now that we know *when* we're going to do it, why don't you tell us *what* it is we're going to do?"

Bruno grinned diabolically. "We're going to rig up his trailer with fireworks and scare him the rest of the way out of his saggy diapers!"

A babble of protest rose up.

"It's perfect," insisted Bruno. "Everyone at Scrimmage's gets to see what a little baby their hero really is, Golden and Dinkman freak out, which takes the heat off me sneaking into the movie, and we knock the Rear Admiral down a couple of notches."

"Those fireworks aren't ours," Boots pointed out. "They belong to the girls."

"Cathy and Diane want them to be used on Cutesy Newbar. *We're* going to use them on Cutesy Newbar."

Larry shook his head. "It's a great idea, Bruno, but we just can't. Rockets and Roman candles and stuff — that's dangerous. We could really hurt the guy, or even ourselves. Fireworks are tricky."

"I know," agreed Sidney. "My dad gave me a sparkler once, and I wound up in the hospital."

"What happened?" asked Mark.

"I swallowed it."

The chorus of laughter that followed was interrupted by Bruno's serious voice. "Come on, guys. I know fireworks can be dangerous. That's why we're going to have an actual scientific genius on the scene telling us *exactly* what to do."

All eyes turned to a lone figure eating quietly at the end of the table. Studious Elmer Drimsdale continued to take slow bites of his salad, oblivious to the fact that he was the centre of attention.

At last, he looked up and regarded his tablemates through thick glasses that gave him an owl-like appearance. "Yes?"

Bruno slapped himself in the forehead. "Sheesh! How can such a smart guy be so out of it? Pay attention, Elm. Now, could you hook up a bunch of fireworks to scare someone without hurting him?"

"I suppose I could if I wanted to." He regarded Bruno intently. "Do I want to?"

Bruno laughed. "You can hardly wait!"

* * *

Boxes of fireworks were handed out the window of room 306 and passed along a human chain out onto the deserted campus. Finally, each hefting a carton, Bruno and Boots climbed out and joined Pete, Wilbur, Larry, Sidney and Elmer.

Mark was on the scene, too, not helping, but recording the event on videotape.

"Get that camera out of my face," threatened Wilbur darkly, "or be prepared to eat it."

Undaunted, Mark focused in on Bruno and Boots and continued to shoot.

"Come on, Mark," said Bruno. "You're doing a documentary on the movie. What's this got to do with *Academy Blues*?"

"This shows our reaction to the film company," Mark insisted. "It'll give my project a new dimension."

"Get real," protested Boots. "You're going to hand this in! It's not about the movie; it's about who blew up Jordie Jones's trailer! Mr. Foley shows it to The Fish, and we all get expelled!"

Mark shook his head. "It's too dark. They'll just see your silhouettes."

"And hear our voices," added Larry.

Mark shook his head. "No sound. I'll use music. Something eerie. Maybe a synthesizer — "

"Or a funeral march if The Fish finds out," added Boots uneasily.

Elmer was wide-eyed, his expression balancing terror and outrage. "We're violating the curfew!" he hissed at Bruno. "You never said we were going to be breaking the rules!"

Bruno stopped. "I didn't? Oh, by the way, Elm, we'll be doing this after lights-out, okay?"

"Well, this is unacceptable!" Elmer stormed, his crew cut standing up even more than usual. "I can't break the rules! If we're caught, we'll be *punished!*"

"Hey, that's no problem," said Bruno airily. "I never get caught."

This statement was greeted by a chorus of sarcastic laughter from the other boys.

"Dishes get washed around here," grumbled Wilbur, "garbage gets picked up, leaves get raked, snow gets shovelled — all because you 'never' get caught."

"So why are you all here?" Bruno challenged.

"Haven't you figured it out yet?" asked Boots, half in exasperation and half in amusement. "We're here because talking you *out* of something is ten times more work than actually *doing* it!"

Elmer folded his arms in front of him. "Well, I'm going home. Remember, Bruno, you signed a contract promising not to do this to me anymore."

"Sure, Elm," said Bruno pleasantly. "Of course, you realize that without your help we're going to kill that poor kid and probably burn down the school. But hey — a contract is a contract."

Elmer looked beseechingly around the group for help, and then finally up to the sky, but nothing was forthcoming. Bruno had gotten him again. With a heavy sigh, he followed along with the rest toward the east lawn. They made a wide circle around the encampment of trailers to avoid the movie security people. Then, well past the small caravan, they doubled back to the furthest camper, the one with the star on the door.

"This is beautiful!" breathed Mark, crouching on his knees and shooting upward. "I've got your heads marching past the full moon!"

36

"How'd you like to go there?" growled Wilbur. "One way!"

Elmer took a small plunger and a coil of wire out of a shopping bag. From his pocket he produced a freehand map scribbled on the back cover of the *Science Gazette*. It showed the trailer and where each rocket, Roman candle, pinwheel, burning schoolhouse and screamer should go. The boys studied the diagram and split up to deploy their weapons.

"Make sure the stuff is hidden," whispered Bruno. "We'll set it off when Cutesy goes to bed tomorrow night, so it'll be sitting around all day."

"What if it rains?" asked Larry. "Fireworks are useless if they get wet."

Elmer scanned the sky, holding up a finger to judge the wind. "Impossible," he decided. "Our weather will be dominated by a high pressure system for at least another thirty-six hours."

No one questioned this. All the boys knew that it had come from an expert.

Bruno grabbed one of the boxes, and he and Boots scurried to the front of the camper. There they set to work, booby-trapping and camouflaging as per Elmer's instructions.

Bruno was smiling and humming as he hid a tall Roman candle in some high grass.

"Shhh!" Boots hissed nervously. "Someone'll hear us! They've got security people, remember?"

But nothing could spoil Bruno's mood. "I know it's going to be harmless, but just the thought of blowing up Cutesy Newbar — I love it!"

Elmer appeared and surveyed their work critically. "Very good," he approved. "Move that pinwheel a little further from the window. Excellent." He began tying the wick of each piece of fireworks to a long cable that snaked in a large circle around the trailer.

Boots was curious in spite of himself. "How will that work?"

"When someone pushes the plunger," explained Elmer, "a sharp electric pulse will shoot through this low-impedance detonator cable, creating a spark that will ignite each of the wicks. That way, everything can be set off at the same time from the same location."

"Elmer, you're a genius," Bruno approved.

As Elmer moved on to the side of the camper where Wilbur and Pete worked, Bruno opened up his jacket and pulled out the biggest rocket of them all. It was half a metre long and striped like a barber pole. On the casing was written *Super-Duper Jumbo-Boomer*.

"Hey, wait a second," protested Boots. "That wasn't on Elmer's plan."

Bruno tied the wick to the main wire as Elmer had done. "This is my own personal birthday gift to Cutesy Newbar. You know, kind of a thank you for letting me wear his orange juice. This baby's going to part his hair right down the middle!"

"Is it safe?" asked Boots worriedly.

Bruno placed the long tube in a hole in the ground so that the top cone wouldn't show above the grass. "What's one little rocket?"

"Yeah, but that's a" — Boots squinted in the dim light — "Super-Duper Jumbo-Boomer."

Bruno laughed diabolically. "It's for a *big* star. He deserves a *big* boom. A super-duper jumbo boom."

"Well, don't you think you should ask — ?" Boots froze. Panic suffused his face. "What was that?"

Both boys were silent. Someone was moving inside the trailer.

"Oh, no!" moaned Boots. "If Jordie Jones hears us and calls security, we're toast!"

"Shhh!" Both boys stood still as statues, listening to the footsteps inside. There was another sound, too, lower, and muffled. Almost like — sobs?

Curiosity got the better of Bruno. Careful not to make any sudden noises, he rose and peered in the camper's front window.

"Are you nuts?" croaked Boots. But Bruno silently waved him over. Knees shaking, Boots joined his roommate and looked inside.

The interior looked like a miniature version of Disneyland — space-age furniture, kitchen, video recorder, stereo, library, exercycle — the works. Jordie Jones sat on the plush couch, watching a movie on the wide-screen TV. Only his eyes weren't on the set. He was hunched over, cradling his head in his arms, his shoulders shaking with distress. The star, one of the best-known faces on earth, the most successful adolescent in the history of Hollywood, was *crying*!

Bruno and Boots exchanged looks of sheer disbelief.

What could Jordie Jones possibly have to cry about?

And suddenly Bruno was tapping lightly on the screen.

Boots almost died. "What are you doing? Cut that out! Aw, I can't believe this!"

But Bruno only knocked harder. "Uh — excuse me," he whispered inside. "Uh — hey, Cutesy."

Startled, Jordie regarded the face in the window, his eyes red, his cheeks damp. He seemed very different without the public smile of jaunty confidence he usually wore. Tonight he could have passed for any one of the seven hundred Macdonald Hall boys.

"Are you okay?" asked Bruno with genuine concern. "What's the problem?"

"Nothing," said Jordie in embarrassment. "Really."

Bruno regarded the actor's tear-streaked face skeptically. "We're coming in," he decided, removing the screen and hoisting himself through the window.

"No!" hissed Boots, shaking his head vigorously. But Bruno was already reaching out to help him inside. Breathing a silent prayer, Boots followed his roommate into the star's trailer.

Jordie thought fast. "I was — uh — rehearsing."

"I thought this movie was supposed to be a comedy," said Bruno.

"A comedy-drama?" suggested the actor hopefully.

Bruno thought it over. "I don't think so. Let's face it — you were bawling. And when a guy with all that money and all that fame and all those girls is crying, it means one of three things: you're stupid, you're crazy or you've got some real problems."

Boots was horrified. "Bruno!" Were you allowed to say stuff like that to a big movie star?

Jordie smiled wanly. "Maybe it's a little of all three. Hey, I know I've got no reason to complain. I've got a great life." He frowned, and for a moment it looked as though he might start crying again. "It's — great — "

"You're not selling me on it," said Bruno.

Jordie looked uncomfortable. "It's nothing. I'm bored."

"You're lying," amended Bruno. "You've got the most exciting life I know."

"I'm lonesome!" the actor exploded suddenly. "I'm always stuck by myself! It's driving me nuts! I know *hermits* who spend less time alone than I do!"

"How could you be lonesome?" Boots blurted out. "Everybody in the world is trying to get near you!"

"Yeah, but nobody ever does! It's like dying of thirst in the middle of the ocean! Here I am, at a place that has seven hundred guys my age, and the only people I ever meet are over fifty. Seth's nice enough, but to him I'm just another prop, like a chair or a bike. Goose thinks I'm going to die if I don't get sixteen hours of sleep a night. And everybody else worries about keeping their jobs and making sure *Academy Blues* doesn't run over budget."

"You're the big star," said Bruno. "Just tell them you need a little more entertainment."

"I tried that," sighed Jordie. "They took me to meet the mayor. He gave me a tour of City Hall and two tickets to the opera. I faked sick."

"Good idea," approved Bruno, looking at the actor with a newfound respect.

"Now, you guys have really got it made," said Jordie with envy. "I mean, tons of friends all living together, eating together, doing things together — "

"You talk like it's a country club!" exclaimed Bruno. "This is a school, with teachers, and classes, and rules. And punishments. While you're living in a mansion and cruising along

Sunset Boulevard in a stretch limo, we're busting our humps in the trenches, doing homework."

"I have to go to school, too, you know," said Jordie defensively. "They get me a tutor."

"It's not the same with a tutor," snorted Bruno. "A tutor works for *you*. You're the boss. He gives you too much homework — you fire him. I can just see me firing The Fish. I've already got dishwashing and confinement. And that's only because they threw me off garbage picking. Beheading is probably next."

"Garbage picking?" Jordie stared at Bruno in sudden recognition. A wide smile of pleasure spread across his face. "I know you! You're the guy who sneaks into the movie!"

Instantly Bruno was on his guard. "Maybe I am, and maybe I'm not."

"Sure you are!" the actor exclaimed. Then, noticing Bruno's expression, he added, "Don't worry. I won't turn you in. It's the highlight of my day to see what you'll try next. That bush was sheer genius!"

"Oh, you liked it, eh?" Bruno preened. "I put a lot of thought into it."

"But why?" asked Jordie. "What's such a big deal about being in *Academy Blues*?"

"I like to think I have a certain flair for the dramatic," said Bruno pompously.

"Besides," added Boots, "he blabbed to everybody he knows about how he was going to be in it."

"Not everybody," put in Bruno.

"Everybody!" Boots insisted. "His folks, all of us, his friends

back home, the entire population of his town — "

"But they're just going to cut you out," Jordie told Bruno.

"They can try," said Bruno grimly. "Dinkman can cut me out of a thousand scenes; I'll still sneak into a thousand and one. And that means, for one shining instant, even if it only lasts a second, I'll be a movie star just like the great Cutesy Newbar."

Jordie blanched. "I'm never going to live that down, am I?"

Bruno shrugged. "It's a trade-off. You're a superstar. And when I take off my pants, I'm not revealing a registered trademark. Welcome to Macdonald Hall, Cutesy. I'm Bruno; he's Boots."

They shook hands all around.

"I know why you're depressed," ventured Boots timidly. "Everybody forgot your birthday, right?"

Jordie looked up in surprise. "How did you know?"

"The whole world has memorized your buns," said Bruno. "How can you be surprised that someone knows it's your birthday tomorrow? Besides, there are three hundred girls across the road who are making a career of you. No offence, but I think they're overdoing it a little."

The actor looked glum. "My parents'll phone, but they're both on business trips, and the few friends I do have are in California. And I don't want to tell Seth or Goose, because they'll call in the national magazines — good P.R. for the picture."

"So?" said Bruno. "It sounds great."

"Don't you get it?" exclaimed Jordie. "Promoting the movie isn't fun. It's part of my job. Nobody celebrates a birthday by *working*!"

Bruno looked thoughtful. "You know what you need, Cutesy? A few hours of hanging out with the guys. And you're in luck. Guess what tomorrow is?"

"We already know it's his birthday," said Boots.

"Poker night!" declared Bruno in his deepest voice.

"Aw, not poker night!" moaned Boots. "Remember what happened last time? Wilbur bet all his peanut butter on three kings, and when he lost, he practically trashed our room! And then Sidney got a royal flush and threw up his arms and dislocated both shoulders! He started screaming, and The Fish raided the game!"

"You mean Mr. Sturgeon?" said Jordie. "What happened?"

Bruno shrugged. "We had to write these thousand-word essays on the evils of gambling. But you wouldn't have to. You've got a tutor. Want to come?"

Jordie looked almost pathetically eager. "It sounds great!" His face fell. "But Goose has insomnia, and on some nights he gets up and looks in my window. If he saw I was gone, he'd think I was kidnapped, or murdered, or something."

"That's a bummer," said Bruno. "Well, there's got to be some way out of it. We've got the magic of Hollywood on our side." He looked from Boots to Jordie, and back to Boots again. "So, Boots, you're not up for another poker night."

"Ever!" Boots agreed with conviction.

"Well, then, that's it," said Bruno with a wide grin. "You sleep here in the trailer, and Cutesy comes to poker night. If you keep your face away from the window, all Goose sees is a blond-haired kid asleep."

"A body double!" agreed Jordie excitedly.

"Now, wait a second — " Boots began.

"It's all settled," said Bruno. "Now it's time to tell the other players about poker night."

Jordie looked at his watch. *"Now?"*

Bruno nodded. "I don't want you to take this personally, Cutesy, but it just so happens that there are six guys outside booby-trapping your trailer." Jordie just stared at him. "No, don't try to figure it out. It was a bad idea, and I'm real sorry." He went to the window. "Pssst! Guys! Take away the explosives. Poker night instead. My room. Tomorrow."

* * *

Mark filmed Pete, Larry, Sidney, Wilbur and Elmer as they carefully picked up the fireworks and replaced them in the boxes. Since they had arranged the various rockets, Roman candles, pinwheels, burning schoolhouses and screamers according to Elmer's diagram, now they followed that sheet again. Removal went much faster than deployment. In twenty minutes, all the pieces were safely back in their cartons — all except one.

Bruno's Super-Duper Jumbo-Boomer had never been on Elmer's map. It wasn't supposed to be where it was, so no one knew to take it away. The big rocket still sat, pointed at the trailer, after the boys had stolen silently back to the dormitories. Its cone top just barely showed, peeking furtively out of the tall grass.

Chapter 4

Body Double

A sheet was jammed under the door to keep the light from room 306 from spilling out into the hall, and a dark blanket hung over the window as a blackout curtain. A deck of cards sat in the middle of the floor, the centre of a circle consisting of Wilbur, Larry, Sidney, Pete and Mark, his video camera at his side.

"How does poker night count as part of your dumb documentary?" demanded Pete.

"It's vitally important," Mark explained. "The star at play. I can intercut it with scenes of Jordie Jones hard at work."

"I don't get it," grumbled big Wilbur, applying a generous dollop of peanut butter to a stack of Ritz crackers. "Yesterday we spent two hours rigging the guy's trailer to go off with him in it, because he's Public Enemy Number One, and tonight we're having a poker game in his honour."

"Sometimes I think Bruno's crazy," nodded Larry.

"Sometimes, I think he's *not* crazy," amended Wilbur. "The rest of the time, I *know* he is. I mean, he put *Sidney* in charge of the birthday cake!"

"I resent that," said Sidney haughtily. "The cake is safe and sound and hidden in the bathroom. It's better than having *you* to look after the cake. That's like hiring a fox to guard your chicken coop."

At that moment, the blackout curtain was nudged aside, and in climbed Bruno, followed by Jordie Jones. Mark filmed furiously.

Pete stared. "Hey, that's Jordie Jones. I thought you said we were waiting for Cutesy Somebody."

"Guys," began Bruno, "say hello to our newest pigeon."

Handshakes were exchanged all around, and the circle was expanded to include Bruno and the newcomer.

"I can't believe it's you!" exclaimed Mark. "I mean, you're so famous! What are you doing *here*?"

"This is the deal," said Bruno. "When he's with us, he's not a big star. He's just one of the guys. Right, Cutesy?"

"Right," agreed the actor. "Only please call me Jordie."

"How's Boots doing at the trailer?" asked Larry.

"Actually, he seemed kind of nervous," Jordie began. "like when he begged us not to leave — "

"He's got it made in there!" scoffed Bruno. "How many of us get to sleep on a king-size waterbed?"

"Will you guys shut up and start taking this seriously?" demanded Wilbur. "Food is about to change hands here! Now — I brought peanut butter and crackers and potato chips. What have you guys got?"

Money was not accepted at poker nights — all bets had to be edible. Mark produced an unopened package of chocolate chip cookies; Larry had cheese and half a loaf of French bread;

Sidney had two bags of marshmallows (smushed, of course); and Pete had a watermelon and three packs of Tic Tacs. From under his bed, Bruno brought out a jumbo bag of rippled potato chips. And then it was Jordie's turn.

The star looked uncomfortable. "Gee, I don't have any great stuff like that. I just brought the leftovers from dinner." From a plastic bag he pulled out two Maine lobsters, sliced prime rib, filet mignon and one half duck *à l'orange*.

Wilbur's eyes bulged. "Hurry up!" he croaked, grabbing the cards and dealing wildly. "If one bite of that spoils, I'll kill myself!"

"Hold on," said Bruno. "First comes the cake. Sidney?"

Stepping in Wilbur's crackers, Sidney hopped off to the bathroom and returned with a large chocolate cake. Instinctively, all the Macdonald Hall boys ducked, but Jordie flushed with pleasure as Sidney carefully placed the plate in front of him.

They all stared. Inscribed in white icing were the words:

Happy 5th Birthday
Angelino Plumbing and Electric

"I've got to get this!" crowed Mark, focusing on the lettering.

"And you thought you were all alone!" laughed Bruno. "Somewhere there's a bunch of plumbers and electricians celebrating with a 'Happy Birthday, Cutesy Newbar' cake!"

Striking a match, Sidney began lighting the red birthday candles.

Larry cocked an eyebrow. "Those are funny-looking candles. Where'd you get them, Sidney?"

Sidney pointed. "From that box under the bed."

Bruno choked. "Under the bed?! Those aren't candles! They're — "

He was interrupted as the firecrackers on Jordie's cake began to explode. The boys dove for cover as the room crackled with small explosions, and chunks of icing and cake flew in all directions, hitting walls and furniture.

"Awesome!" breathed Mark.

Jordie pulled a large candy rose from his famous blond hair. "Man," he said with reverence, "it's a good thing I'm not turning forty-five!"

"What's going on in there?" came Mr. Fudge's voice from out in the hall.

Bruno mouthed the word "Hide!" He shoved Jordie into Boots's bed as Larry and Sidney both dove under it. Wilbur disappeared into the closet with the food and the cards, and Pete hustled Mark, filming all the way, into the bathroom, where both lay flat in the tub.

In one brilliant athletic move, Bruno turned out the lights, grabbed the blackout curtain with his right hand, the sheet under the door with his left, and leapt into his bed, already snoring.

There was the sound of a key in the lock, and the door swung wide, revealing Mr. Fudge, the Housemaster, in his pyjamas. He shone a flashlight on Bruno's bed.

"Walton — O'Neal — have you got the radio on? I could swear I heard a machine gun!"

"I don't know anything about that, sir," said Bruno, stretching and yawning.

"How about you, O'Neal?" barked Mr. Fudge. "What do you

have to say about this?" The flashlight shifted to Jordie.

The star pulled the covers right up over his face. He thought furiously back to Boots — a soft voice, well-spoken, more nervous than Bruno's.

"I'm not sure, sir," came Boots's voice from the pile of covers. "I was asleep."

The flashlight switched off. "You boys settle down in here." The door closed. They heard the Housemaster's footsteps going down the hall to his own room, and then the closing of that door.

Boys began to come out of the woodwork, crowding around Jordie Jones.

"That was fantastic!" said Larry. "You sounded exactly like Boots!"

"Yeah!" agreed Pete. "For a second I thought Boots had come back."

Even Bruno was impressed. "You know something, Cutesy? You've got talent."

"Hey," said Sidney suspiciously. "Where's Wilbur?"

Six pairs of eyes darted around the room. Wilbur was nowhere in sight. Then they heard chewing noises from the closet, along with the loud crack of a lobster shell being broken open.

Bruno wrenched the closet door open. There sat Wilbur, prime rib in one hand, a lobster claw in the other.

"I got hungry," he mumbled, his mouth stuffed.

Bruno folded his arms. "That's Cutesy's poker money! You have to give him the equivalent in crackers before we start playing!"

Wordlessly Wilbur motioned toward his peanut butter and crackers, indicating that Jordie should help himself. By this time, Sidney had sliced up the watermelon, and Larry was nibbling at the cheese. Mark opened up his chocolate chip cookies, and Pete was making a potato chip sandwich on French bread.

With a sigh, Bruno ripped open his chips. "Forget poker," he mumbled, cramming his mouth full. "Let's hit the chips."

* * *

A dozen girls crouched in Miss Scrimmage's apple orchard, receiving instructions from Cathy Burton. The group was dressed in black pants and black sweaters, and their hair was stuffed under wool caps. They looked like what they were — an assault force.

"Now, we've got to be really quiet," Cathy was saying, "because there's this guy with a lopsided toupee and white pyjamas who hangs around Jordie all the time. We can't let him stop us."

"Do we tell Jordie we're giving him a birthday party?" asked Wilma Dorf.

"It's a surprise party," answered Diane. "If we told him, it would spoil the surprise."

"And no talking," ordered Cathy. "This is a silent mission. We get in, grab him, and get out. Anyone who messes up dies. Okay, let's move."

Commandos on a raid, the girls hopped the orchard fence, stole across the highway and moved like shadows over the darkened Macdonald Hall campus towards the east lawn and their idol.

In front of the trailer, all twelve girls flattened themselves to the ground. Cathy reached up and tried the door. Locked. From underneath her cap, she produced a tiny hairpin and tossed it to Diane, who set to work at the keyhole. There was a click, and the camper door swung wide.

The raid was as swift as lightning. All twelve poured into the trailer, pounced on the figure lying in the bed, wrapped him like a mummy in his own blankets and sprinted back to their campus, holding their prize like a battering ram.

At the wrought-iron fence surrounding Miss Scrimmage's, the commandos formed a human conveyor belt, passing their captive up, over and down. They ran straight in the front door and along the main hall to the cafeteria. There waited the entire student body, some three hundred girls, a sea of Jordie Jones T-shirts and party hats.

Cathy rasped. "We've got him!" It was a whisper and a scream all rolled into one.

What would have been a roar of anticipation was scaled down to a mighty hiss from many throats. Then three hundred voices began whispering "Happy Birthday To You," along with applause in mime.

As they headed into the last chorus, the commandos lovingly placed their bundle on the floor and watched expectantly as it began to writhe and unravel.

"Happy birthday, dear Jor-die . . ."

The cocoon burst open, and out peered a pyjama clad Boots O'Neal.

"Happy birthday to — aaagghhh!"

"Boots, you idiot!" wheezed Cathy. "Where's Jordie?"

Boots shrugged miserably. "It's poker night."

"Why didn't you tell us it was you?" demanded Diane.

"Well, you didn't exactly give me a chance!" Boots tried to defend himself.

Cathy slapped her forehead. "Well, this is typical! You let a man do something and he ruins it!"

"Me? I was sleeping!"

But his protest fell on deaf ears. The girls were booing and hissing and pelting him with party hats. Ruth Sidwell dumped the birthday cake over his head, and Vanessa Robinson added the contents of the punch bowl. Then the angry and disappointed girls began to file out in a dignified and orderly fashion.

"But I didn't do anything!" Boots sputtered plaintively.

Cathy was unsympathetic. "Let's face it, Melvin. You screwed up." She and Diane joined the line of exiting girls.

"You can't leave me here!" Boots quavered.

"You think about that," advised Diane coldly, "the next time you try to pass yourself off as Jordie Jones!"

Showering punch-soaked cake to the cafeteria floor, Boots staggered after them, trying not to scream. "Wait! Wait! Come back!"

But the girls were gone, and he was trapped in the middle of the night at the wrong school, in his pyjamas, looking like he'd just been run over by the Good Humor man. This, he reflected, was what always happened when you did what Bruno told you to. Sure. Sleep in the trailer. Who'll know the difference? Heaving a deep sigh, he began to wander the halls, hoping to find the front door.

Suddenly he felt a nudge in the small of his back. He wheeled to find that this nightmare was a sunny day at the beach compared to what faced him now — Miss Scrimmage, her gigantic and often misfired shotgun aimed at his belly.

"Hands up!" ordered the Headmistress.

Somehow she hadn't noticed that her entire student body was throwing a party, but she had managed to corner him.

Boots reached for the sky.

* * *

By two o'clock in the morning the first poker hand got dealt, but by then the food was all gone, so there was nothing to bet with. Wilbur and Larry were in a spirited argument over whether a straight beat a flush, and Sidney sliced his hand open on the jack of diamonds, bleeding all over Pete's cards. Mark abandoned the game to film the crisis, and that was when Bruno decided it was time to call it a night.

"This was a great party," he pronounced happily. "I don't know if it beats Hollywood but, Cutesy, you're welcome any time."

"Just bring more of that lobster," added Wilbur, full to bursting.

"This is the best birthday I ever had!" Jordie declared with conviction. "Thanks a million!"

Bruno opened the window. "Just kick Boots out and send him home."

A demented shriek cut the air. "Call security! Call the police! Call the coast guard! J.J.'s *gone!*"

"Oh, no!" moaned Jordie. "That's Goose!"

"But you're here," said Pete in perplexity. "That means someone's kidnapped — "

"Boots?" finished Bruno. "Who'd want to kidnap Boots?"

Larry's voice was anxious. "Maybe — well — what if they thought they were kidnapping Jordie Jones?"

Wilbur stuck his head out the window. "There are lights on at Scrimmage's. Oh, no — Miss Scrimmage has somebody! She's marching him back to the Hall!"

Bruno followed Wilbur's pointing hand. "Boots!"

"Macdonald Hall to the rescue!" exclaimed Jordie, really getting into the role of being a student.

"Are you nuts?" cried Bruno. "You've seen too many movies! That's Miss Scrimmage! We were better off with kidnappers! She's armed to the teeth!"

"Get out of my way!" Grabbing his camera, Mark was out the window and sprinting across the campus.

"Mark — no!" cried Bruno. "If you scare her with that camera, she'll shoot Boots! Awww — "

Out of options, Bruno hurled himself out the window and raced toward the south lawn. The rest of the boys, Jordie included, followed.

"Mr. Sturgeon! Mr. Sturgeon!" howled Bruno. "Wake up, sir!" He roared up the steps of the small wood-frame cottage and began pounding on the door. "Mr. Sturgeon! Quick!"

After a moment, the door opened, and the Headmaster appeared, slightly dishevelled, wrapped in a red silk bathrobe.

"Walton, it's after two in the morning," he said angrily. In some confusion, he spied Jordie among the boys standing behind Bruno. "What is the meaning of this disturbance?"

"It's Boots, sir! I mean Melvin! I mean O'Neal!"

"I know the boy to whom you are referring," said the

Headmaster irritably. "What about O'Neal?"

"He's been captured by Miss Scrimmage!"

"Good Lord!" exclaimed Mr. Sturgeon. He hit the porch running, his slippers flapping loudly, and took off in the direction of Miss Scrimmage's.

The scene was chaotic. Mr. Sturgeon led the boys in a sprint for the highway while Goose Golden ran around the east lawn, waking up all the movie people. Lights were flashing on in all three dormitories, and pyjama-clad boys appeared, investigating the cause of the ruckus. They were greeted by the sight of their dignified Headmaster in full flight, his bathrobe flowing behind him like Batman's cape.

"Go back to bed at once!" he tossed over his shoulder. "Everything is under control!" He cupped his hands to his mouth. "Miss Scrimmage, put down that weapon this instant!"

But the Headmistress continued to wield her trusty shotgun, prodding Boots with righteous indignation. "March, you villain, you beast! How dare you terrorize my students?"

Quaking in his filthy pyjamas, Boots complied.

The two parties met in the middle of Highway 48.

Mr. Sturgeon's face was bright red from outrage and the exertion of his run. Bereft of speech, he reached out, grabbed Boots and shoved him forcibly into the crowd of boys bringing up the rear. Then he snatched the shotgun by the barrel, wrested it from Miss Scrimmage's hands and popped out the shells. In a remarkable display of strength for a man of his years, he bashed the gun against the pavement until the stock shattered and the mechanism flew in all directions.

"How dare you?" shrilled Miss Scrimmage. "I need that to protect my poor innocent girls from marauders like *him*!" She glared at Boots.

Mr. Sturgeon had never been so angry. "Madam, I warned you what would happen if you ever pointed that thing at one of my boys again! Consider yourself vastly fortunate that it is not *you* lying dismantled on the highway instead of your weapon! You have my solemn vow that if I ever see you in possession of a firearm at any time in the future, I shall assemble witnesses, have you declared a danger to the public safety and see you clapped up in jail! Now" — he drew himself up to his full height and pointed imperiously toward Miss Scrimmage's school — *"go!"*

Gathering the shreds of her dignity, Miss Scrimmage retreated.

Still smouldering, Mr. Sturgeon turned his murderous countenance on his own students just in time to see Mark Davies lowering his camera in awe and triumph. His steely grey eyes fell on Jordie.

"Jones," he said with deceptive calm, "please take yourself off and assure your manager that you are not dead. His caterwauling is disturbing the county."

Jordie ran off to calm Golden.

The Headmaster turned to Boots and the veterans of poker night. "The rest of you have until eight o'clock this morning to formulate an explanation for this night's extracurricular activities — which I will hear in my office at that hour. And let me assure you, it had better be magnificent!"

* * *

"Mildred, don't you dare touch that phone."

It was after 3 AM, and the telephone in Mr. Sturgeon's kitchen was ringing.

"But it might be Miss Scrimmage, dear. The poor woman must be terribly upset."

"Let it ring," said the Headmaster grimly. "If she is merely upset, you may assure yourself that she got off easy."

"Oh, William, don't be insensitive," coaxed his wife. "Miss Scrimmage is no longer young, you know."

"And I'm sixteen, I suppose," said her husband dryly. "Your sympathy is misplaced, Mildred. Sympathy begins at home."

"That's charity, dear."

"Don't correct me. I used to be an English teacher. Of course, now I specialize in disarming deranged women." The ringing stopped. "Thank heaven. Perhaps now she'll have the decency to go to bed so we can all get some sleep."

There was a persistent rapping at the door.

Mr. Sturgeon stood up and retied the sash of his bathrobe. "If that's Walton and O'Neal, they will be packed and gone by sun-up."

"Oh, dear," she said soothingly, "don't do anything you're going to regret."

On creaking legs, the Headmaster stepped to the front door. "At this point, Mildred, my only regret is answering the ad for a teaching position at Macdonald Hall more than thirty years ago." He flung the door wide. "This had better be good!"

There on the porch stood Jordie Jones. "Mr. Sturgeon, may I have a word with you?"

"My door is always open," said the Headmaster, looking pointedly at his watch.

"Thank you." Jordie allowed himself to be led to the kitchen. "Ma'am," he acknowledged Mrs. Sturgeon politely, "I'm so sorry to be disturbing you."

"Oh, my goodness, it's Jordie Jones!" she exclaimed. "I'm one of your biggest fans!"

"Thank you," said the actor.

"Well, Jones," said Mr. Sturgeon, "might we get to the point? It's rather late. Or early, if you prefer."

"It's just that you can't punish Bruno and Boots."

Mr. Sturgeon raised an eyebrow. "Do tell."

"See, tonight was all my fault," Jordie explained. "It was my birthday, and I was totally depressed because my parents are away on business and all my friends are in L.A. So Bruno and Boots threw me kind of a party. But we had to leave someone in the trailer because of the way Goose is, and we picked Boots because he's got blond hair and he's about my size."

"Why, I think it was just wonderful of Bruno and Melvin!" enthused Mrs. Sturgeon. "Such dear, thoughtful boys!"

"They're great," Jordie agreed. "But from then on, things got kind of crazy, because some of the girls from across the street kidnapped me. At least, they thought it was me. But it was really Boots. And then came the lady with the gun — but you were great, sir! You went in there with no thought for your own safety! You could get a medal for what you did!"

Mr. Sturgeon coughed away an insane desire to giggle, convinced that a hundred medals would not cover his heroism since Walton and O'Neal had arrived at Macdonald Hall.

"Well, Jones, I appreciate the input. It does show the events of tonight in a different light." He stood up. "However, I must insist you remember that our boys are bound by many rules and regulations to which you are not subject. Now, do you wish for our students to leave you alone to your work?"

Jordie turned pale. "Oh, no!"

"Then, while you are socializing, you will consider yourself temporarily a student here and behave accordingly. Is that acceptable?"

Jordie leapt to his feet joyfully. "Are you kidding?"

"The proper response, Jones, is 'Yes, sir.'"

"Yes, sir!"

"Fine," said the Headmaster. He consulted his watch. "You are presently violating the curfew by five and a half hours. You will return to your trailer and go to bed."

"Not until you sign my autograph book," said Mrs. Sturgeon brightly.

Smiling, Jordie reached for her pen.

Chapter 5

Getting into Character

Mark Davies manipulated the zoom on his video camera and focused in on the *Academy Blues* crew.

"I screened last night's footage. I've got the most amazing angle of The Fish bashing up Miss Scrimmage's shotgun. Wait till you see his face!"

Pete looked thoughtful. "Maybe you could blackmail him."

Boots laughed mirthlessly. "That's probably the only reason why we're not all expelled. I can't believe he didn't punish us."

Bruno nodded. "I've got a theory about that. I bet Cutesy went to him and took the heat for us. When you think about it, all we did was violate curfew. Most of the blame goes to Cutesy, Miss Scrimmage and the girls. And even Cutesy was sort of a victim."

"*I* was the victim," said Boots accusingly. "None of you guys got kidnapped, beaten up, drowned and marched at gunpoint."

"And you missed a great snack," added Wilbur. "These movie people really know how to eat."

"Hey, what are you doing here, Bruno?" asked Larry. "I thought you had to stay away from the east lawn."

Bruno shrugged. "I was sent for. They want me in this next scene, so The Fish said I could come." He looked pleased. "I told you I'd get into the movie."

Seth Dinkman was pushing through the crowd towards them, with Jordie Jones at his side.

"Okay, Walton, congratulations. You're in this scene." The director gave Bruno a dirty look. "You can thank your friend Jordie for that. If it were up to me, I wouldn't have you on my set unless I was filming *Jaws V* and I needed someone to play shark bait."

The cameras were focused on a remote corner of the campus, where a deep, muddy trench had been dug. Two actors, dressed in plumbers' overalls and hip boots, were in the hole, working on a section of sewer pipe.

Bruno was flushed with excitement. "You're the greatest, Cutesy!" Jordie flashed him the thumbs-up sign.

"Okay," said Dinkman, "you extras stand here with Jordie, watch the plumbers and look amazed. No words, no gestures. You're watching something that you don't see every day." He backed out of the scene and called "Action!"

"Cut!" yelled Bruno.

Dinkman was confused. "Who said that? Who yelled 'Cut'? Only I yell 'Cut.'"

Bruno raised his hand. "Uh — Mr. Dinkman, sir — Cutesy here isn't following instructions. We're supposed to look confused, and he's grinning."

"Don't worry about Jordie," said Dinkman. "He's got different instructions. You just worry about yourself. And don't yell 'Cut' on my set, got it?"

"Well, why is he smiling?" Bruno persisted. "Why isn't he confused, too?"

"Because he just isn't, okay? All right — action!"

"Cu— I mean, stop — hold it," called Bruno.

"Bruno — " whispered Jordie warningly.

Dinkman was turning purple. "What is it now?"

"Well, it's just that I have to know why we're confused and he's not, otherwise I can't get into my character."

"You don't have to get into your character!" roared the director. "The scene lasts seven seconds!"

"Look," said Jordie, "here's how it goes. This is a ruptured sewer pipe, and we're watching these guys fix it."

Bruno was insulted. "And my character is too stupid to know that a ruptured sewer pipe is funny?"

"No, no, no," said Jordie. "Listen, *Academy Blues* is about a guy who goes to boarding school and really hates it. That's me. I've been stuffing things down the toilet for three weeks now, trying to bust up the plumbing."

Bruno snapped his fingers. "The grapefruit thing."

"The point is," Jordie went on, "I've finally succeeded, which is why I'm smiling. But you guys don't know about it, so you're confused."

"Are you motivated now?" rasped Dinkman.

"Well, no," said Bruno. "I mean, you left out the part where this pipe breaks. How could it already be dug up if it hasn't busted yet?"

"It is busted," explained Jordie patiently. "We just haven't shot that scene yet. But in the finished movie, it'll all be in order."

"Why don't you just shoot it the way it's supposed to be?" asked Bruno.

"Because we're shooting it with a stuntman, and he isn't here yet, the lucky sonofagun!" shrieked Dinkman. "You've got ten seconds to get ready for the scene! If you're not ready, *you're gone*!"

"Bruno," hissed Jordie urgently, "on a movie set the director is king. You can't argue with him. Even I can't argue with him. Paul Newman wouldn't be able to argue with him. If Zeus came down from Mount Olympus and ended up here, he'd have to keep quiet and listen to Seth. That's the way it is."

Bruno snorted. "Then Dinkman is a great name for him. He's a dink, man!"

"Okay — action!" The cameras rolled. "Cut! *Cut!*" Dinkman bounded onto the scene, close to hysterics. *"You!"* he screamed into Bruno's face. "You're smiling! You're supposed to look confused!"

"Well," Bruno explained, "if I'm with Cutesy, he and I are probably friends. So I wouldn't be confused. He would have told me."

"Get off my set!"

* * *

In the hockey rink, Coach Flynn was winding down another practice of the Macdonald Hall Macs. The season was almost over, except for the annual game between the Macs and their archrivals, the York Academy Cougars.

Finally the coach blew his whistle and called the players to centre ice. "Team," he said, "I know we didn't do very well this year. But we can still save our self-respect by giving it our best shot against York next week. Yeah, they've got a better record than we do, but it's our home ice, and we've got a great shot at it."

The boys all banged their sticks enthusiastically on the ice.

"Will the girls be coming over to cheer us on?" asked Pete Anderson, the goalie.

Mr. Flynn looked embarrassed. "I don't think you'd better count on them. Relations are a bit — uh — strained between our two schools."

Larry nudged Bruno and Boots. "Miss Scrimmage is suing The Fish for the price of the shotgun, plus fifty thousand bucks mental cruelty," he whispered.

"That's enough, Wilson," said the coach sternly. "Now, I just want you boys to keep your emotions high for one more big game. Do us proud. Okay, a few more laps and hit the showers."

As Captain Boots O'Neal led the team, first clockwise and then counterclockwise around the ice surface, Bruno spied Jordie, leaning on the boards, watching. Working up the biggest head of steam he could muster, he streaked toward the sidelines and stopped on a dime, digging his blades into the ice. A shower of snow covered the actor.

Jordie brushed himself off, laughing. "It's a good thing Goose didn't see that. Pneumonia is one of his favourite fears."

"So," said Bruno, "how's my buddy Seth cooling off?"

"Pretty good," said Jordie. "He took all the footage with you in it and had it burned. They're all over there roasting marshmallows right now."

"I still say I was right," Bruno insisted.

"The director is always right," Jordie corrected, "even when he's wrong." He looked longingly at the ice. "I haven't skated in years."

"Yeah? You guys skate down in California? I thought you just surfed."

"I always wanted to play hockey," said Jordie. He shrugged sadly. "I wanted to play anything."

"So why didn't you?"

"Are you kidding? Goose even hides my tennis racket! He once caught me playing touch football, and he got so freaked out he tried to have the other players arrested! I'm not allowed to get a black eye, a fat lip, a chipped tooth or any kind of bruise that makeup won't cover."

Bruno watched as Coach Flynn skated off the ice and clumped into the dressing room. Then he scrambled over the boards into the seats, ripped off his skates and handed them to Jordie.

"Okay, Cutesy, let's see what you can do."

Delighted, Jordie laced on the skates, stepped onto the ice and tried a few experimental strides. "This is great!" he called. "It's like riding a bike! You never forget!"

Wump!

"Oh, no!" whooped Bruno. "You landed butt-first! There goes the career!"

Back on his feet, Jordie began to move around the rink, gaining speed as he boosted his confidence. The other Macs gathered around him, shouting encouragement.

"Maybe we should put you on our team," said Boots sadly.

"We need all the help we can get against York Academy. They were third in the province this year."

Wilbur pulled off his helmet and shook his head. "The only player who could win us this game wears a red S on his chest and is able to leap tall buildings in a single bound."

Pete slapped his stick into his heavy goalie pads. "And what good is home ice advantage when the girls aren't even going to be here to bug the other team?"

Skidding across the ice in a pair of high-tops, Bruno joined the group. "I'm more worried about the dance Friday night. I mean, if The Fish and Miss Scrimmage are at war, they may just call it off."

Larry shook his head. "He was thinking of cancelling, but in the end, he's going to let us go. I overheard him say to Mrs. Davis that we need to let off steam, what with the excitement of the movie and all."

The far-off look was once again in Jordie Jones's world-renowned eyes. "A dance. I'd sure love to get in on something like that."

Boots stared at him. "You? Are you crazy? Those girls would tear you to pieces in five seconds! You might as well just jump into a tank filled with piranhas! You should have seen them the night they got me!"

Jordie tried a quick stop, almost losing his balance. "Yeah, I know. But still, it would be great. Would you guys believe I've never danced with anybody before?"

"Wait a second," said Wilbur. "I saw you in a movie dancing with this girl in a huge ballroom, and I remember thinking you were the luckiest kid alive."

Larry snapped his fingers. "I saw that, too. Man, she was beautiful!"

"Who cares about *her*?" scoffed Wilbur. "In the background you could see the most amazing buffet! The dessert table alone was a monument — like the pyramids!"

Jordie dismissed this with a wave of his hand. "That doesn't count. I was *working*."

"Nice work if you can get it," grinned Larry.

"Just because it looks like I'm enjoying myself in a movie," said the actor, "doesn't mean I really *am*. I mean, when I dance with someone, or kiss someone, it isn't *fun*. I approach it the way you guys might solve a math problem."

"You mean wrong?" asked Pete, confused.

"Like a job. I'm getting paid, the girl's getting paid, the sixty technicians watching us are getting paid and we all work together to make the scene as real as possible. But a *dance* — no script, no crew, just people dancing because they *want* to — " His face fell. "Boots is right. It's impossible."

"Remember the science-fiction movie where you danced with the three-headed alien girl to steal the nuclear code to break your parents out of a tritium cell?" Pete inquired. "Well — do three-headed aliens get more money than normal actors?"

Bruno looked thoughtful. "You know," he began slowly, "maybe you couldn't go to Scrimmage's as Jordie Jones, but what if you were somebody else?"

"I don't get it," said Larry. "How could he be somebody besides himself?"

Bruno grinned. "With the magic of Hollywood."

"Hey — this doesn't involve me sleeping in a trailer, does it?" asked Boots warily.

His roommate ignored him. "Cutesy," he asked the star, "do you have any connections in makeup?"

Chapter 6

The Royal Sneeze

On Friday night, the lights shone in the makeup trailer long after Seth Dinkman had stopped the day's filming. A single cosmetics expert laboured over a young client.

Finally the door opened, and the boy stepped out onto the dark campus, waving his thanks inside. But instead of heading to the heart of the village of trailers on the east lawn, he ventured off to the Macdonald Hall dormitories. He entered the third building and walked through the crowded hallway, receiving only a few curious glances. Approaching room 306, he reached out and knocked smartly.

"Yeah?" came Bruno's voice from within.

"Sir," replied the boy formally, with just a trace of an accent, "is this the address at which one must present oneself for participation in tonight's social activities?"

Bruno threw the door open and stared in shock. "Holy cow! *Cutesy*? No way!"

Boots appeared over his shoulder. Awed, he merely whispered, "Jordie?"

The figure in front of them looked almost nothing like Jordie

Jones, the famous actor. His fair complexion had been darkened with makeup, and his blond hair was completely covered by an authentic silk turban. Although he wore his regular clothes, the look was completely different, because shadow had been applied to soften the chiselled features of his face. He looked plumper, rounder. But the *pièce de résistance* was the eyes — Jordie's famous baby blues were now a dark, dark brown.

He bowed formally. "At your service."

"But your face!" Boots stammered. "Your *eyes*!"

"Contact lenses," the actor replied in his normal voice. "And the turban is left over from *Redhead in Arabia*. I figure we can tell the girls I'm the son of some sheik or prince or something."

"With that accent, they'll never know it's you," promised Bruno in awe. "Come on, it's time to go."

Most of the three-hundred-odd Macdonald Hall senior students were swarming on the front lawn, just beginning to trickle across the highway to Miss Scrimmage's. Not wanting to be among the first to arrive, Bruno, Boots and Jordie hung back by the flagpole. There they met Wilbur, Larry, Sidney, Pete and Mark. Elmer never went to school dances, as his throat always closed up in the presence of girls. Tonight he was focusing his telescope on a small pulsar in the constellation Cygnus and ignoring the whole thing.

Taking his place in the group was slight, skinny Calvin Fihzgart. This was Calvin's first school dance, and he had proclaimed himself the world's greatest ladies' man for the occasion.

"Those chicks had better watch out!" he declared, spraying

his body liberally with cologne. He already smelled like the wreckage of an exploded perfume factory. "There are going to be a lot of hearts broken tonight!"

Boots pointed at Calvin. "What's he doing here?"

Larry shrugged. "He just showed up and started babbling. I think he's nervous about his first dance."

"Nervous? Are you nuts?" roared Calvin. "I just hope I don't get any jealous boyfriends coming after me!"

Bruno clamped his hand over the lens of Mark's video camera. "Aw, come on! How does *this* fit into your dumb documentary?"

"It's very important," said Mark righteously. "This illustrates what movie stars go through not to be recognized."

"No, it doesn't," countered Boots. "It illustrates who snuck Jordie Jones into the dance, just like it illustrates who played poker with Jordie Jones and who snuck out after lights-out with five boxes of explosives to booby-trap Jordie Jones. And if The Fish sees it, you can expand your masterpiece to include us carrying our luggage to the train station, because we'll all be expelled!"

Wilbur shook his head. "If we get expelled, the only thing he'll film is the inside of his nose, because that's where that stupid camera will be!"

"Don't worry," Mark assured them. "I'll cut out anything that could get you guys in trouble."

"Okay," said Bruno. "We should be fashionably late by now. Let's go."

As they crossed the highway, Calvin pulled out his cologne and gave himself another dousing. This had the boys coughing and covering their eyes. Jordie dissolved into a sneezing fit.

"Hey, Calvin!" choked Bruno. "Give everybody a break, eh!"

Calvin was outraged. "Chicks dig guys who wear after-shave."

Jordie blew his nose. "Not if they can't get within twenty metres of them without passing out," he sniffled.

"Besides," gagged Boots, "you don't even shave."

"No problem!" Calvin enthused. "I rubbed my face with sandpaper so it'd *sting* a little!"

As they melted into the swarm of boys at the entrance to Miss Scrimmage's gym, Larry had nothing but praise for Jordie Jones.

"I can't believe it!" he crowed. "You don't just look different. You've changed into somebody else! Even the way you walk!"

Jordie smiled. "It's a trick I picked up in acting class — each character you portray has his own posture and way of moving. The son of royalty would be stiff and formal."

Bruno was impressed. "Wow. I didn't know you could act. I thought you were just a movie star." He glanced through the sea of bodies into the gym, where the music was starting up. "Remember, blow your cover and you're hamburger."

Jordie nodded intently, and they marched through the door. There sat Miss Scrimmage, resplendent in a frilly ball gown of pink and silver, the school colours. She took one look at Boots and recoiled in horror, rocking back and forth on the hind legs of her chair and almost toppling over. Only Wilbur's strong arm kept her upright.

"How dare you?" shrilled the Headmistress at Boots. "You

thug! You break into my school, prowl about at night, terrorizing my poor defenceless girls and now you expect to come here to socialize? My eyes may be old, young man, but my nose can still smell a rat!"

Boots studied the floor.

"But Miss Scrimmage," protested Bruno, "Mr. Sturgeon said he could come."

"Mr. Sturgeon?" she blurted without thinking. "What does that old coot know about discipline?"

"A good deal more than one might expect," came a dry voice behind her.

From the refreshment table appeared Mr. Sturgeon, in his hand a cup of punch, on his face his coldest fishy expression. This he turned on his hostess. "I daresay I am exercising a fair amount of *self*-discipline right at this moment."

Miss Scrimmage pointed at Boots. "Why has this hooligan not been properly punished?" she demanded.

"I conducted an investigation," said the Headmaster darkly, "and concluded that the blame lay elsewhere. O'Neal is a registered student of Macdonald Hall. You will accept all my students, or you will accept none of them."

Miss Scrimmage flushed bright red with anger. Mr. Sturgeon had her cornered. She had to back down, or she would be spoiling the dance for her own students.

She beamed. "Who is this absolutely charming young man?"

She was looking straight at Jordie Jones. Quickly the actor stepped behind Wilbur.

"Yes, you," the Headmistress persisted. "The handsome boy in the turban. Are you new to Macdonald Hall?"

Stepping out from cover, Jordie nodded uneasily and managed to look shy. Mr. Sturgeon regarded him quizzically.

"How lovely," said Miss Scrimmage. "Where are you from?"

Boots's heart sank. The Headmaster knew every one of his students by face and by name. There was a big difference between bluffing Jordie Jones through one little dance and making up crazy stories right in front of Mr. Sturgeon. The Fish was no dummy, and if he caught them in an outright lie, it would take a lot more than the magic of Hollywood to save them.

"He's foreign!" Boots exclaimed suddenly. It was the truth. Jordie Jones was an American citizen, and in Canada, that made him foreign. If they could somehow get through this without *actually* lying, The Headmaster might go easy.

"Yes, but from where, specifically?" Miss Scrimmage inquired. *"Where — is — your — home?"* This she said slowly and with a lot of volume, as though Jordie would not understand English very well. Boots concentrated on the actor. Come on, Jordie, don't lie, don't make up some weird country with a bizarre name, don't blow it . . .

"Altadena," replied Jordie.

No! Boots wanted to scream. *That's it! That's the lie! It's all over!* But then he remembered his California geography. The towns around Los Angeles had all different types of names, from Spanish to Arabic. Maybe Altadena was the suburb Jordie was from. Cautiously, Boots risked a glance at Mr. Sturgeon. The Headmaster was still intent on Jordie.

"Altadena," the Headmistress mused. "I don't believe I'm familiar with . . ."

"On the one side is the desert," said Jordie, beginning to warm to his role. "On the other, the sea."

Boots smiled to himself. California, all right.

"How wonderful," declared Miss Scrimmage. She rose, holding up her hands for quiet. The music died. "Girls," she announced, "we have a very special visitor, all the way from the distant land of Altadena. Please welcome — " She looked at Jordie. "I'm so sorry. I'm afraid I neglected to ask your name."

"We may not speak it," replied Jordie, dead serious.

The Headmistress did a double take. "Are you — royalty?"

Bruno put an arm around Jordie's shoulders. "Let's just say that millions of people know him and love him."

"Your Highness!" exclaimed Miss Scrimmage, dipping into a low curtsey. "Girls!" she cried. "This boy is a prince in his home country!"

"Miss Scrimmage," said Mr. Sturgeon quickly, "perhaps we should allow the young man an evening away from all the attention."

"Yes, yes, of course." She curtseyed her way out of their path. "It is a great honour, Your Highness. An honour and a privilege. Our school will always remember this day . . . "

She continued to rant and rave as the Headmaster led them into the gym. As soon as the music came on again, he turned to face the actor in the turban.

"Jones, what is the meaning of this?"

"Shhh, sir!" hissed Bruno. "If the girls hear you, we'll have a riot on our hands!"

"Perhaps you should have considered that possibility when you concocted this absurd scheme," returned Mr. Sturgeon.

"Well, sir, we didn't think anybody would recognize him. How did you do it?"

The Headmaster sighed. "The makeup is excellent, the voice and mannerisms convincing. But *think*, Walton. Who else could he possibly be?"

"I'm sorry, sir," said Jordie, shamefaced. "It's just that I've never been to anything like this before. But you're right. I'll leave."

Mr. Sturgeon regarded the movie star's downcast eyes. Here was a boy who had what every child — and a good many adults — only dreamed of, yet he was the loneliest boy in the world. He had fame and fortune, but the simple things — friends, school dances, a normal childhood — were out of his reach. In a strange way, the Headmaster felt sorry for him.

"I don't think Miss Scrimmage could stand the loss of prestige that your departure would bring about," he said sardonically. "You may stay for now, Jones. But if you feel that someone suspects your true identity, however slightly, you must leave immediately. Is that clear?"

"Yes sir!" grinned Jordie, and ran off in search of someone to dance with.

Bruno faced his Headmaster. "That's a wonderful thing you just did," he said heartily. "You know, sir, you're a really nice guy!"

Mr. Sturgeon stared furiously at him, his steely grey eyes burning twin holes in Bruno's cheeks. Then he adjusted his chaperone's button and walked away, fuming.

Bruno shrugged, annoyed. "You give a guy a compliment, and he bites your head off."

Boots pointed to Wilbur, who was attempting to cut the line for the buffet table. "Come on. Let's eat while there's still something left."

They waited patiently in line as Wilbur ravaged the selection of cold meats and cheeses, mounting up a quadruple-decker sandwich so big that Mark recorded it for posterity on video-tape.

"Stay away from the chicken salad. It's deadly!" Bruno and Boots wheeled to see Cathy and Diane bearing down on them.

"Well, well," Bruno greeted them. "The Cutesy Newbar Fan Club."

"Hey," said Cathy. "What's the deal with this kid in the tur-ban?" She pointed to Jordie, who was dancing with one of Miss Scrimmage's younger students.

"Exchange kid," said Bruno. "In his home country he's some kind of prince."

Cathy shrugged. "Prince Schmince. He's a creep."

"He's a nice guy," put in Boots.

"It's all a matter of charisma," Cathy lectured. "He doesn't have any. Now, take Jordie Jones, for instance. Jordie with a bag over his head would still have more charisma than that guy."

Bruno and Boots stared at Cathy and then at each other.

"Look," said Diane. "Here he comes."

The song had ended, and Jordie was on his way over. Bruno jazzed up the introduction to the girls, calling the stranger, "Your Most Exceedingly Royal Majesty," "Great One" and "Beacon for All Humankind."

"You'll have to forgive us for not being totally blown away

by your royalness," Cathy told the newcomer flatly. "We're pretty big Jordie Jones fans, and he's right across the street."

"Ah," said Jordie. "I understand he is a very fine actor."

"Actually," giggled Diane, "he can't act for beans. But with a face like that, who needs talent?"

Jordie was taken aback.

"Don't get us wrong," put in Cathy. "We love him. We love his movies. It just doesn't have anything to do with acting, that's all."

* * *

By nine o'clock, the dance was going at full force. The lights were low, and the girl acting as DJ had replaced Miss Scrimmage's disc, *Great Dance Tunes of the Forties and Fifties*, with the one Bruno had slipped her — Electric Catfish's *Filet of Fire* album. Bruno and Boots were dancing with Cathy and Diane and, a short distance away, Jordie was paired with Vanessa Robinson. Mark circulated on the crowded dance floor, sticking his video camera into everybody's business.

Calvin Fihzgart still hadn't found himself a partner and was so distraught that he had taken to bopping up to groups of girls who were dancing together. This created a traffic jam on the floor, since everyone was moving in the same direction — away from Calvin. Soon gyrating bodies were packed like sardines on the left side of the floor. On the right was Calvin, all by himself, boogying his heart out.

Something was going wrong, and for Calvin there was only one possible explanation. His aftershave must have worn off. Without interrupting his dancing, he pulled out his bottle of cologne and gave a mighty push on the plunger. But because he was moving at fever pitch, he missed his face. A large perfume cloud drifted straight over his shoulder and settled around Jordie and Vanessa, two metres away. Vanessa covered her face, but Jordie caught a snootful. He began to sneeze violently.

Suddenly, over the heavy pounding beat from the loudspeakers, came the half-demented voice of Cathy Burton. *"Stop! Stop the music!"*

There was an eardrum-popping scratch and then silence. Cathy surveyed the room like a bounty hunter. "I know that sneeze! That was the sneeze from the pillow-fight scene in *Camp Calamity*! Jordie Jones is *here*!"

There was a gasp, followed by frenzied shuffling as the girls scoured the gym for the source of the sneeze. Then Cathy's eyes fell on the red-faced, runny-nosed royal prince, making his way quietly to the door.

"Freeze!"

Boots grabbed Cathy by the arm and tried to steer her attention from Jordie. "Aw, come on. He's just an exchange student — "

He was interrupted by another loud sneeze. This time there was no question. It had come from the Beacon for All Humankind, and it was a very famous sneeze indeed. The next one blew the turban right off Jordie Jones's head.

Total chaos was the result. A high-pitched shriek rose up in the gym, followed by a stampede for Jordie. There was an incredible crunch as the girls strained to reach him and the boys rushed to protect him. On the floor, Sidney scrambled madly to get out of the way, but he was trampled underfoot. The centre of a giant shoving match, Jordie was buffeted to and fro, unable to control his own movements. Mr. Sturgeon and the other Macdonald Hall chaperones tried in vain to disperse the students, but the girls would not be denied a shot at their movie idol.

"Girls! Go to your rooms!" ordered Miss Scrimmage. "Young ladies do not behave in this unseemly manner! Girls!" Unable to control her star-crazed students, she did the next best thing and fainted right into the reluctant arms of Mr. Sturgeon.

"Hang on, Cutesy!" bellowed Bruno. *"I'll save you!"* He pitched forward, almost losing his balance, then looked down to see a bedraggled figure under his right foot. "Get up, Sidney!" he snapped in annoyance. "What're you trying to do — kill somebody?"

Sidney rolled over, his face bruised and dirty. "Oh, hi, Bruno," he said sleepily. "How come you're way up there?" Suddenly he remembered where he was and sprang to his feet, vaulting up Bruno's back to perch on his shoulders, above the throng.

"Get off me! I'm busy!" Bruno cried. "I'm trying to rescue Cutesy." No sooner were the words out of his mouth than he had the solution. Carrying Sidney with him, he pushed through the crowd to Jordie, who was caught in a tug of war between Wilbur Hackenschleimer and Wilma Dorf.

"Climb on Wilbur!" cried Bruno.

"What?"

"Climb on Wilbur!"

The young actor scaled the big boy like a ladder. There were twin cries — victory from the boys and outrage from the girls — as he seated himself on Wilbur's shoulders, teetering dangerously.

"Oh, boy, this is *great*!" crowed Mark, holding his camera above the sea of students and filming blindly.

Mr. Sturgeon, helpless with Miss Scrimmage fainted away in his arms, could only shout, "Hackenschleimer, be *careful*!"

"Now what?" called Jordie.

"We're going to *die*!" quavered Sidney.

"Exit stage left!" Bruno shouted.

They began to move gingerly toward the gym door, Jordie and Sidney swaying with each step like twin towers of Jell-O. Their progress was slow but sure, and the Macdonald Hall boys began cheering wildly. Led by Larry, a line of blockers formed to clear a path to the exit.

"Ten feet to the door!" cried Jordie excitedly. "We're going to make it!"

But the way was blocked by one last obstacle. There, in front of the exit, teetered another human skyscraper — Cathy, on top of Diane.

"Hi, Jordie!" Cathy waved. "Remember me?"

"Terrific!" muttered Wilbur under his breath.

"Aw, no!" moaned Bruno. "Come on, Cathy, give us a break!"

The opposition stood its ground, ready to do battle.

"All right, you asked for it!" steamed Bruno. *"Ramming speed!"*

"No!" shrieked Sidney.

Mark climbed onto the buffet table for a better camera angle.

Gritting his teeth in determination, Bruno stepped boldly forward, but Diane deftly spun around him and moved in on Wilbur. High above the floor, Cathy made a grab for Jordie, who pulled away, tipping himself backward. For one agonizing moment, he hung there, waving his arms frantically to regain his balance.

"What's going on up there?" cried Wilbur, feeling himself being pulled back.

"That's it," groaned Bruno in resignation. "We're dead!"

At last, the actor could remain upright no longer.

He and Wilbur went down like a house of cards. At the last second, Jordie reached out and grabbed the rim of the basketball goal by the wall. Wilbur fell heavily to the floor. Jordie hung on the hoop, feet dangling above the crowd.

"AAAAAAAAGH!!!"

The bone-chilling shriek silenced the entire gymful of people. There at the far entrance stood Boots with Seth Dinkman, Goose Golden and three burly security guards. It was not hard to locate the source of the scream. The manager's face was the colour of an overripe tomato, standing out like a sunrise against the white of his clothes.

Cathy jumped down from Diane's shoulders. "Boots brought the cavalry," she said dejectedly. "That guy's getting to be such a *nuisance*!"

By this time, Miss Scrimmage had revived and was moving under her own power, so Mr. Sturgeon stepped forward with his customary air of command and declared the dance officially over. The three security men set about getting Jordie down from the basketball hoop.

"Mr. Sturgeon," called the star as soon as his feet touched the floor. "Could I talk to you for a minute?"

"Yes, I know," said the Headmaster wearily. "This is all *your* fault."

Seth Dinkman spotted Bruno and cast him a look that would have melted lead. "Stay away from my star!" he rasped. "Stay away from my crew! Stay away from my movie! Just *stay away!*"

Bruno watched him storm out the door, fuming. "Boy," he said mildly. "What a crab."

The procession of Macdonald Hall boys crossing the highway back to their own school was in agreement on one thing: The dance had been a major success.

"It was great," agreed Pete. "But there's one thing I just can't figure out. Who was that guy with the towel on his head?"

Chapter 7

Fred the Goalie

". . . And then he gave me the fish eye and said, 'Walton, if you can honestly say to my face that smuggling the Jones boy into the dance *wasn't* your idea, you will walk out of this office with no punishment whatsoever.'"

A few boys were sprawled comfortably on the grass watching the movie set decorators building a three-metre-high model of the Faculty Building.

"He let you off scot-free?" asked Sidney incredulously.

"Nah, I confessed. You know what it's like when you're face-to-face with The Fish. You think up all these great lies, but the words won't come out of your mouth."

Boots shuddered. "We should be grateful we got off as easy as we did."

"How's this?" said Pete, reading from a steno pad he'd been working on. *"Dear Miss Scrimmage, How are you? I am fine."*

"What kind of stupid letter is that?" exploded Mark. "We're supposed to be apologizing for wrecking the dance."

"I'm working up to that part," said Pete. "Besides, I didn't do anything to her stupid dance. I didn't even know that prince guy was Jordie Jones."

"If you had stayed here with me, none of you would be in this predicament," said Elmer seriously. Since Mark was busy writing, Elmer had been called into service to keep the videotape rolling for the documentary.

"Just keep shooting," said Mark irritably. "Hey, what are you doing?" Elmer now had the camera pointed up at the sky. "The film crew's over there, remember?"

"Yes, but there's a very fascinating formation of cumulonimbus clouds — "

"This isn't a documentary about clouds! I *have* to have footage of them building that model!"

"What do they need a model of the Faculty Building for, anyway?" put in Pete. "They've got the real thing right here."

"Because it has to blow up at the end of the movie," Mark explained. "Remember?"

"I'm with Pete," grumbled Wilbur, his letter to Miss Scrimmage already smeared with Cheez Whiz. "Let them blow up the real one."

"You guys complain too much," said Bruno. "You just put, *Dear Miss Scrimmage, Sorry we trashed your dance. Better luck next time, Yours sincerely*, and sign it. It's better than having to sit through a dull dance. This one was the best ever!"

"No one minds a little excitement," said Boots. "Within reason. It just stings to have to write an apology when any idiot could see that the riot was caused by Cathy, Diane and the girls."

"The Fish is just trying to calm Miss Scrimmage down," said

Larry. "After last night, she bumped up her lawsuit by another twenty-five G's."

"Yeah, well, tell The Fish I'll testify," said Boots feelingly.

"I can't understand why those girls go so crazy when they see Jordie," commented Sidney, checking the security of his assorted Band-Aids.

"They're in love with him," said Larry.

"So what?" challenged Boots. "My mother's in love with my father, but she doesn't bust up the house every time he comes home from work."

Bruno shrugged. "They're sick."

"It makes you think, though," said Mark. "I always dreamed of being a big star like Jordie Jones. But that poor kid lives like a prisoner. He can't even go out to a third-rate dance."

"Without turning it into a *first-rate* dance," laughed Bruno.

"Mark's right, you know," said Boots thoughtfully. "What good is it to have looks, talent, money and fame if you can't go out of the house to enjoy it because some nut like Cathy is going to tear you limb from limb?"

Bruno was skeptical. "Before you rev up the pity party, just remember that if Cutesy didn't like all this stuff, he could just quit. He's pulling in millions! And don't forget, he gets to be in the movies."

"And you don't," Boots laughed. "I knew we'd come to that part sooner or later."

"It's not over till that film crew's packed and gone."

"You'd better hurry," Larry reminded him. "We've got nothing but hockey practice until the big game, and then comes the wilderness survival trip."

Bruno covered his face with both hands. "I forgot! This is our term for Die-in-the-Woods!"

"And by the time we get back, *Academy Blues* will be done," added Boots.

"Well," said Bruno, "I'll just have to figure out some way to get excused."

"Are you kidding?" exclaimed Larry. "*Nobody* gets out of Die-in-the-Woods! I've seen The Fish hold back diplomas for guys who missed it. They actually had to *come back* just to go on the trip!"

"Hah!" said Bruno. "Sidney got delayed once before he finally went."

"That was pure luck," Sidney put in. "I broke my leg."

"See?" said Bruno. "It's that easy."

"The wilderness survival trip is a required element for every student," lectured Elmer, who was back filming clouds again.

"I don't get it," grumbled Wilbur. "All they ever care about around here is grades and averages and academics. Why are they so big on sending us into the bush to *starve*?"

"Wilderness survival has been a tradition at Macdonald Hall since the very beginning," Elmer explained. "And while it is not as important a part of student life as it was in the early days, it is still considered character building and essential to a well-rounded education."

"Says who?" said Bruno.

"Says The Fish," supplied Boots. "And the Board. And our folks. We'll go, and we'll get it over with, and we'll shut up about it. It could even be fun."

"Marvin Trimble went in the fall," said Wilbur pessimistically, "and he told me the food was terrible!"

Mark stood up and grabbed the camera from Elmer's hands. "Give me that! You're taking clouds again!"

Bruno finished his letter, but his mind was decidedly elsewhere. "I guess I'll just have to get into the movie before the trip."

* * *

The dining room table in the Headmaster's cottage gleamed with the very best linen, silver and china. Mrs. Sturgeon passed the salad dressing to Seth Dinkman, who was on her right. "And how is the movie coming along, Mr. Dinkman?"

"Pretty good," replied the director. "We're a couple of days behind schedule, but the cast and crew are just starting to get into a rhythm."

"Oh, it's a musical," said Miss Scrimmage. "How lovely."

Goose Golden brayed a laugh right into her face. "Hey, that's a good one. A musical. Yeah, that's funny."

The Headmaster glared at his wife across the table. This dinner party had not been his idea, and he was especially irritated by the presence of Miss Scrimmage. Mrs. Sturgeon smiled back warningly.

"My girls love music," Miss Scrimmage rattled on. "It is one of their accomplishments."

"Yeah?" said Goose unkindly. "What are the others — demolition? Guerilla warfare? *Ninjitsu?*"

"Hey, Goose," said Dinkman quietly. "Cool it."

"But they almost killed J.J.!"

Miss Scrimmage bristled at Golden. "How dare you, sir? I'll have you know ours is a finishing school!"

The manager snorted into his plate. "Well, if that's a finishing school, I'd hate to see what they've got down at the women's prison!"

Mrs. Sturgeon stood up. "Why don't we all have dessert?" She disappeared into the kitchen.

"I'll help," said Mr. Sturgeon and swept out in her wake. He faced his wife over the kitchen counter. "Congratulations, Mildred. Bringing those two together at one table was a social masterstroke."

"Oh, William, stop your complaining and hand me those plates."

He took the dishes from the cupboard and placed them on her tray. "What's for dessert — nails?"

"I wish you would take these gatherings a little more seriously," she scolded. "Tonight is a wonderful opportunity for you and Miss Scrimmage to sort out your differences."

"She is far too busy creating new ones with Mr. Golden. I wonder how much she'll sue *him* for. He must be wealthier than I. That toupee alone is worth, at minimum, ninety-nine cents."

"Shhh! Be nice. Everyone will be much more cheery when they've had some coffee and kiwi flan. You'll see."

At that moment, Miss Scrimmage's shrill voice reached them.

"You, sir, are a *cad!*"

And by the time the Sturgeons returned to the dining room with dessert, Seth Dinkman was sitting alone at the table, looking embarrassed.

"Oh, dear!" said the hostess. "Where is everybody?"

"Perhaps Miss Scrimmage invited Mr. Golden to step outside," suggested the Headmaster dryly.

Dinkman laughed. "The lady took off in a snit. And Goose — well, he can get kind of crazy where Jordie's concerned. He went to his trailer to cool off. Sorry." He craned his neck at the tray. "Hey, is that kiwi flan? My favourite!"

Dessert was served, and Mrs. Sturgeon watched happily as Dinkman downed his portion, then Miss Scrimmage's and Golden's as well.

Mr. Sturgeon cleared his throat carefully. "Perhaps it's just as well the others have gone. It gives me an opportunity to discuss young Jones."

"Jordie? Sure. What do you want to know?"

"No doubt you are aware of his complicity in that unsavoury incident at Miss Scrimmage's last night."

Dinkman shrugged. "These things happen around a star. People go nuts. And I've got to say Jordie handles it a lot better than some actors I could name who are twenty years older than him."

"No doubt," said the Headmaster. "In fact, if he could disguise his sneeze as well as he disguises himself and his voice, last night might never have happened. The point is, Dinkman, Jones is not just an actor; he is a young boy, and I know the species well. Remember, you're not on location in the Sahara Desert. There are seven hundred other boys here, showing Jones exactly what he's given up for the sake of success."

"Maybe," Dinkman conceded. "But Jordie makes pictures at ten million bucks a pop. That ought to be enough to keep him in line."

"To an adult mind, yes; on a headmaster's salary, definitely. But to Jones, I doubt it. He's merely human. He wants what he doesn't have."

Dinkman frowned. "Are you saying I should keep him away from your kids?"

"Just the opposite," Mr. Sturgeon replied. "He should be given the freedom to socialize fully whenever he's not working or taking lessons with his tutor. If he can enjoy these normal friendships whenever he chooses, it won't be necessary for him to pursue them at four o'clock in the morning, or dressed as the Maharajah of Rajputan."

Dinkman thought it over. "Maybe you're right — of *course* you're right. But it has nothing to do with me. I don't care what Jordie does when he's on his own time. But Jordie's parents hired Goose and put him completely in charge. And let's face it, Goose is an idiot."

Mr. Sturgeon smiled sardonically. "I wasn't going to mention it if you didn't."

Dinkman polished off his coffee. "Are you kidding? You think I'd let Goose on my set if I didn't have to? Every time I ask the kid to do something, *he* butts in and we have a contract negotiation. It's murder!"

Mr. Sturgeon looked skeptical. "But surely, as director, your authority is considerable."

"So is Goose's mouth." He pounded the table with determination. "I know what I'll tell him. I'll say the kid isn't performing well on the set because he's unhappy. Then I'll drop a few hints about cutting the star's salary. Poor old Goose won't know if he's coming or going." He grinned. "It might even be fun."

* * *

The Macdonald Hall Macs were running breakaway drill on
Pete Anderson, the goalie, when a second netminder in full
equipment took the ice. He skated to the opposite goal,
assumed his stance and began to bang his stick on the crossbar.
The challenge.

Boots nudged Bruno. "Who's that guy?"

Bruno squinted at the unfamiliar mask and shrugged. The team
had no backup goalie, and the custom was to dress one of the
defencemen in the event that Pete couldn't play. "Who's missing?" he asked, surveying the line of shooters. "Maybe Larry?"

"No," said the office messenger from behind him. "I'm over
here."

"Who cares? Let's smoke this guy!" Sidney Rampulsky
snared a puck and streaked down the ice towards the mystery
goalie. About three metres in front of the net, the blades of his
skates lost the ice. He fell heavily, spinning on the seat of his
hockey pants into the boards. The puck slid slowly into the
goalie's stick. The mystery man celebrated his save wildly.

Laughing, Boots grabbed another puck, roared in and picked
the top corner of the net with a lightning wrist shot.

Jordie Jones ripped off his mask. "Showboat!"

Bruno skated over. "Get that mask back on, Cutesy! You
want Coach Flynn to see you?"

Jordie covered his face. "So how do I look?"

"Like a dead man if your manager catches you."

"That's the weird part," said the star. "When I was through
for the day, Goose told me to take off and have a good time.
Just like that."

Boots looked surprised. "He probably didn't mean hockey."

"For sure," Jordie agreed. "Actually, he looked like he didn't mean any of it. He was sweating, and his voice sounded higher than normal, and he kept looking over his shoulder at Seth. And then, as I was walking away, I heard him say his mantra. He only meditates when he's really freaking out." He shook his head. "It doesn't make sense, but I wasn't going to hang out until he changed his mind. I knew you guys were practising, so I came here. And when I saw the spare equipment, I couldn't resist it."

"Good thing you're a goalie," said Bruno. "The coach won't be able to tell it's you."

"Okay," called Jordie, backing into the net, "do your worst!"

A second line of shooters formed, but the identity of the new goalie was soon passed from helmet to helmet, and the skaters each lobbed slow, gentle shots at the net.

Jordie easily turned aside the first few, then called time and glided over to the line of attackers. He flipped his mask up and faced them, eyes blazing. "The next guy who gives me a weak little baby shot gets his head separated from the rest of his body!" He waved his stick like a battle-ax, and returned to the net.

Shrugging, Wilbur Hackenschleimer fired a hard slapshot past Jordie. Larry scored. So did Sidney, although the force of his shot put him out of control. The puck beat Jordie to the left side and, a split second later, Sidney himself got past the goalie on the right, sliding headfirst into the net.

Then Jordie stopped one, pulling a high wrist shot out of the air with a lightning glove. Calvin Fihzgart scored, but the actor foiled Rob Adams and Mortimer Day. He even outsmarted Boots, who made a quick fake, pulled the puck to his backhand and flipped it toward the net. Jordie followed the move perfectly, making a blocker save. Next was Bruno. He made a charge directly at the goalie. There was a head-on collision then, as the two lay in a heap, Bruno reached out with his stick and pulled the puck into the net.

"What was that for?" Jordie demanded.

"Second effort," explained Bruno.

A whistle blew. "Walton, what are you doing?" Coach Flynn stood at centre ice, glaring in their direction. Bruno and Jordie scrambled to their feet. The coach stared at the newcomer. "And you are . . . ?"

Before Jordie could reply, Bruno announced loudly, "Who, him? Uh — well, Coach, it's so obvious. This is — Fred."

Flynn's brow furrowed. "Fred?"

"Yes, sir," continued Bruno, leaping in with both skates. "We told him how tough it's going to be against York on Saturday, and how we only have one goalie to drill with, and because he's got school spirit and homework's light, what with the big trip coming up, he volunteered to stand in goal during practice. What a guy." He put an arm around Jordie and looked at centre ice hopefully.

Coach Flynn thought it over. Finally, he said, "Good idea. Thanks, Fred."

"Glad to help out," came a gruff voice from behind the mask. It was Jordie's best guess as to what Fred the goalie would sound like.

The practice continued, with Pete and "Fred" in goal. After

half an hour, the coach called all the skaters together for some drills, and Pete worked with Jordie on basic goaltending moves.

"What are we going to do if Flynn ever gets around to asking himself Fred Who?" Boots whispered to Bruno during the passing exercise.

"You think too much, Melvin," was Bruno's response. "The coach is tearing his hair out worrying about the game. He wouldn't care if Cutesy was from Neptune, so long as he helped to prepare for York Academy."

* * *

By a coincidence, every time Jordie Jones was finished early on the set that week, "Fred" happened to have light homework and would come to play goal at hockey practice.

Coach Flynn was pathetically grateful. After a terrible season, the team was finally coming together, and an extra goalie at practice helped immeasurably. Two netminders instead of one meant that twice as many players could be actively involved in the drills, instead of standing around waiting.

As a goalie, the actor was only so-so. He was very quick with his glove, a holdover from Little League baseball (before Goose had put a stop to his participation, he added). He was also keenly observant, something learned in his experience as an actor, and therefore very difficult to fake. Even Boots, the captain and best player, couldn't fool him. Jordie's problem was the easy shots. Anything that came along the ice, no matter how soft, managed to elude him. Still, he manfully faced every puck, giving his all — even after the embarrassment of letting in a clearing pass from centre ice.

"He's a hard worker," Coach Flynn told Boots. "And he never gives up. Do you think we could convince him to go out for track?"

"Probably not," Boots managed. "Fred's got a lot of — uh — extracurricular things going on."

On Friday, the players remained in the locker room long after their coach's pep talk.

"Coach Flynn's right," said Larry. "We've come a long way this week. I think we've got a good chance."

"York Academy's going to slaughter us," predicted Wilbur mournfully.

"I don't know," said Boots. "It feels like we're starting to click."

"The last game of the season is a dumb time to *start* to click," commented Pete. "But it sure would be nice to give those turkeys a run for their money tomorrow."

A masked head poked into the locker room, and Bruno waved Jordie inside. "Come on in, Cutesy. The coast is clear. How does it feel now that your hockey career is over?"

Jordie smiled. "I'll miss it. But I would've had to stop anyway. Goose noticed this tiny bruise on my arm this morning. It was *nothing*! The makeup people couldn't even find it to cover it up. So now he's gearing up for one of his marathon talks where he just blabs until I can't stand it anymore, and I tell him what he wants to hear."

"Why are you so scared of him?" asked Sidney. "Doesn't *he* work for *you*?"

The actor smiled. "I love Goose. I know I complain about him being a pain and all, but I've worked with the guy since

the old *Cutesy Newbar* days. He's like a second father to me."
He thought it over. "More like an estranged uncle — or how
about an older brother who's kind of weird?"

"Are you coming to see the game tomorrow?" asked Boots.

"For sure!" Jordie nodded enthusiastically. "Seth's agreed to
shoot around me for a couple of hours. I'll be in the front row."

"We'll need all the cheering we can get," said Larry. "The
girls aren't coming. Miss Scrimmage is still steaming over the
dance. She's threatened to bring her lawsuit up to a quarter
million."

"Bummer," agreed Bruno. "The girls were always a great
boost, especially when they used to throw stuff at the other
team. And you've got to figure there won't be a lot of parent
and alumni turnout after our 2 and 7 season. Still, we've got a
movie star on our side. I'll bet those York turkeys haven't got
one of those!"

Chapter 8

Bench Strength

The turnout for the annual hockey game was better than expected. This had little to do with hockey. Parents and alumni were anxious to get a look at the movie crew and the famous Jordie Jones in action. They came from all over Toronto and southern Ontario, and they came early. Although the game was not set to begin until 2, there was a large crowd of spectators on the east lawn by 9 AM.

It brought out the showman in Seth Dinkman. He was engaging in friendly banter with the visitors and plugging *Academy Blues*. Goose Golden circulated, too, handing out Jordie Jones Fan Club applications to everyone under the age of seventy.

Dinkman also made sure to use as many student extras as possible and, after much nagging from Jordie, the name of Bruno Walton was called. There was an enormous cheer from the Macdonald Hall students.

The director was smiling as he put an arm around Bruno's shoulders and led him away from the crowd of parents and boys. "All right, Walton," he said, the friendly grin never wavering. "You're getting one last chance, so don't blow it.

There's a line in this scene, and Jordie wants you to have it."

Bruno was ecstatic. "A speaking part! Wow! You won't be sorry you picked me!"

"I didn't pick you," growled the director, still smiling for the benefit of the crowd. "Jordie did. Now, here's what's happening."

A camera focused on Jordie, dressed in a school jacket, carrying an armload of books.

"Even you can do this," Dinkman instructed. "Jordie's walking along the path. You jog up behind him, tap him on the shoulder and you say, 'Hey, Steve, there's a package for you at the office.'"

"I'm Steve, remember?" Jordie supplied. "It's the character I'm playing."

"Right," said Bruno, a look of intense concentration on his face.

Scene 26, take 1: As Jordie walked, Bruno approached from the rear, slapped him heartily on the shoulder, opened his mouth and said — nothing.

"Cut! *Cut!*" Dinkman rushed over. "Well?"

"I forgot my line," Bruno admitted.

The spectators broke into appreciative applause.

"Listen carefully," the director ordered. "'Hey, Steve, there's a package for you at the office.' Okay?"

Scene 26, take 2: "Hey, Steve," called Bruno, "there's a package for you at the — the — " His face twisted. "That place! With desks — papers — "

Scene 26, take 3: "Hey, there, Steve's a package at the office — "

Scene 26, take 4: "Hey, Steve — uh — got any good packages lately?"

"Cut! *Cut!*" Dinkman bounded onto the scene, red-faced. "Stop laughing!" he barked at his cameraman, who was doubled over.

The crowd chanted, "Bru–no! . . . Bru–no!"

"Quiet, everybody! This is a sound take!" The director turned to Bruno, who was panting and sweating from all the jogging. "Makeup, powder this guy down! He looks like he's just run the Boston Marathon!"

"You know, Seth," said Jordie solicitously, "maybe it would go better if we had a trial run-through."

"Yeah, sure," said the director impatiently. "Go for it. Rehearse. Take your time. It's the pivotal scene in the movie, after all!"

As the makeup technician coaxed the shine out of Bruno's face with a large powder-puff, Bruno practised. "Hey, Steve, there's a package for you at the office. Hey, Steve . . ."

Scene 26, take 5: Everything went according to plan. Bruno jogged, tapped and spoke. "Hey, Steve, there's a package for you at the office — *hic!*"

The smooth professional manner of Jordie Jones shattered into a million pieces. It started as a giggle, but soon grew into a wild cackling. That set Bruno off, hooting and hiccupping.

"*Cu-u-u-u-ut!*" The director was frantic. "One lousy line! We could train a baboon to do it! But not this baboon!" He turned to Jordie. "It's been five takes — eleven minutes — two thousand dollars of the studio's money. Do I have your permission to find a kid who can deliver one stinking line?"

With an apologetic look at Bruno, Jordie nodded.

"Walton," said the director, "don't call us; we'll call you."

"But — *hic* — I was just getting warmed up!"

"And now you're getting cooled down!" snarled Dinkman. "Listen, kid," he continued, not unkindly, "you're not an actor. And every time you come near my set, there's trouble. Face it. You're not going to be in *Academy Blues*."

Bruno looked concerned. "Do I have a pimple? Is it my hair? I can get it cut, you know."

Dinkman clutched at his head. "I thought I was speaking English! It must have been Swahili! Okay, let me put it this way: This is a movie *not* starring you! You're not in it! At no point during the film do you appear! You are conspicuous by your absence! No scenes include you, as all scenes *exclude* you! You are *not there*! Casting, get me another kid!"

Bruno thought it over. "How about I practise all night and we shoot this tomorrow?"

Security had to lead him away from the set, amid a tumultuous ovation.

"Dinkman isn't going to go very far in the movie business," Bruno told Boots. "He has no eye for developing talent. And he's a bonehead besides."

"Never mind," said Boots soothingly. "Pretty soon it'll be time to suit up for the game."

* * *

The bus bringing the York Academy Cougars arrived around eleven-thirty, and the annual hockey luncheon took place at noon.

The York players looked supremely confident and did a lot of bragging about their successful season. The Macs were quiet and very nervous. Bruno in particular smouldered as the Cougars' captain went on in great detail about the glorious victories that had brought his school team to the Ontario semi-finals. Only the presence of Mr. Sturgeon kept Bruno from starting an argument. Even the mild-mannered Boots had his jaw set in grim silence.

Later, in the locker room, Bruno put everyone's feelings into words. "I know they're better than us, but we have no choice. We have to win, just to shut those turkeys up."

"Yeah!" exclaimed Pete with conviction. "Did you hear that captain guy? What a big mouth!"

"And Mr. Hartley just sat there, letting them brag on and on," added Larry. "If we ever pulled something like that, The Fish would probably make us forfeit the game."

"All right, boys," said Coach Flynn. "You're in exactly the right mood, and the Cougars put you in it. Don't get mad; get even."

The players took the ice to the applause of the staff, students, assorted parents and alumni of Macdonald Hall and a small contingent of York fans.

In the front row of seats, right behind the Macdonald Hall bench, sat Jordie Jones, cheering himself hoarse on behalf of his newfound friends. He wore a white T-shirt on which he had written TEAM MASCOT in red permanent marker. That had been Bruno's idea, to counteract York Academy's mascot, Myrtle the cat, a thirteen-kilo grey tabby, who sat on the play-ers' bench looking fat and contented. She was surrounded by her five kittens, now fully grown and almost as big as their mother. They were apprentice mascots Franny, Danny, Manny, Annie and Fanny. It was an anniversary of sorts for them. They had been born during a Macs–Cougars game.

Bruno was satisfied that a movie idol mascot was far more prestigious than a platoon of obese felines. The Cougars thought so, too, and were not pleased.

"Some mascot!" jeered the captain, making a disparaging gesture toward Jordie.

Bruno pointed at Myrtle on the bench. "Some cougar!" he returned good-naturedly.

"Hey, Bruno — over here!" There by the penalty box stood Mark, filming furiously.

"Great idea," approved Bruno. "Now we'll have our game captured on video."

"I'm not here for the *game*," said Mark scornfully. "This is part of my documentary." He turned the camera on Jordie. "The star, rooting for our team! It really brings out the human side of the movie business."

"That video camera really brings out the idiot side of you," commented Wilbur, skating his warm-up.

Boots and the Cougars' captain lined up for the ceremonial face-off, and Mr. Sturgeon and Mr. Hartley dropped the puck. The two players shook hands with each other and both Headmasters, and it was time for the game to begin.

The Cougars came out flying and quickly took the lead with an early goal. The Macs' defence dug in, but in his exuberance Bruno took a tripping penalty. York Academy capitalized on the power play to take a 2–0 lead into the dressing room at the end of the first period.

"Maybe a movie star *doesn't* beat a bunch of cats," panted Wilbur, reaching for an orange.

"They're tough," Pete agreed. "They've got some great shooters."

"We're only two goals back," said Coach Flynn optimistically. "Hang in there, and eventually the breaks will start to go our way."

He was right. Early in the second period, Boots, parked in front of the opposing net, deflected Wilbur's slap shot for Macdonald Hall's first score. The home crowd roared its approval. Behind the bench, Jordie Jones was standing on his seat and screaming.

The Cougars struck back, widening their lead to 3–1. But just before the end of the period, Sidney Rampulsky made a spectacular rush at the net. He tripped and created so much confusion that Larry Wilson was able to pop the puck over the York goaltender with a backhand shot. 3–2, Cougars.

The Macs' dressing room was lively during the next intermission.

"We're in striking distance!" raved Coach Flynn, his face pink with excitement. "We can skate with them and score on them! We've proved it!"

"And we can beat them!" roared Bruno.

When the Macs took the ice for the third period, the crowd noise was deafening. Macdonald Hall could feel an upset in the making. They chanted, "Go, Macs, go!" stamping to the rhythm and rocking the arena.

Bewildered by the strength and desire of their opponents and unnerved by the crowd, the Cougars were totally out of sync.

They fell back against the Macdonald Hall attack and, three minutes into the period, Captain Boots O'Neal found himself with a clear view of the net. He fired a picture-perfect wrist shot that caught the upper lefthand corner. Tie game.

From then on, it was as if the Stanley Cup were at stake. The spectators were treated to end-to-end action, but the score remained deadlocked at 3. Pete and the Cougars' goalie were making spectacular saves as each team strained to take the lead.

As the third period ticked away, the Macs were exhausted, and even York Academy seemed to be tiring. Jordie's voice was hoarse from cheering, his face bright red as he watched the action unfold. Even Mark was impressed by the drama on the ice, and was filming hockey instead of the star.

Boots was grey in the face and gasping as the players lined up for a face-off deep in Macdonald Hall territory. He looked up at the clock. "Two and a half minutes to go!" he wheezed. "If we can hold them off, then we can rest! And it's anybody's game in sudden death overtime!"

"Overtime?!" roared Bruno in outrage. "No way! I can't stick around for overtime! I've got to get into the movie before Die-in-the-Woods!"

"Are you kidding?" panted Larry. "We'll be lucky to *make it* to overtime, let alone win!"

Bruno took his position. "I can't do overtime," he said grimly. "It doesn't fit into my schedule."

The Cougars' centre won the face-off and pulled the puck back to the right defenceman for a slap shot from the point. The boy wound up, and while his stick was still in the air, Bruno swooped down like a hawk and stole the puck. Not a finesse skater, he galloped down the ice, stickhandling with one hand and fending off attackers with the other. By the time he reached the Cougars' blue line, all five York skaters were swarming around him. No single player, nor the combined efforts of all, could move him from the puck.

"Get off!" he yelled, breaking free of the pack and roaring in alone on the goalie. Not much of a shooter either, he concentrated on aim rather than style. First he pulled the puck a complete stick-length behind his body, then part swept, part shovelled and part shot it right through the goalie's legs and into the net.

The crowd went wild. The Macdonald Hall bench cleared, and a joyous procession of Macs descended on Bruno and hoisted him up on their shoulders. As they skated him around the ice, he waved his stick to the crowd, exciting them even further. The referee whistled for order, but order was slow in coming.

As the swarm of Macs passed in front of the Cougars' bench, Manny, the smallest mascot, jumped over the boards and onto the ice in front of them. There was a mad scramble to put on the brakes. As usual, Sidney was the first to stumble. He tripped Wilbur, who knocked Boots off balance and the captain, struggling under Bruno's weight, fell flat on his back in front of the group. That was all it took. It was follow-the-leader on skates. One by one, the Macs tripped over their captain and scattered across the ice. Bruno was last, crunching heavily on the seat of his hockey pants.

Suddenly it was very quiet in the rink. The crowd watched

anxiously as the referee and a few of the Cougars began helping the fallen players to their feet. They all got up, all but one. Pete Anderson lay face down on the ice. He was out cold.

Mr. Sturgeon was out of his seat, over the boards and at Pete's side in seconds, skidding and sliding. Flynn was several steps ahead of him.

"I think he's okay," panted the coach. "He just got his bell rung a little."

The two men sat Pete up against the boards, and Flynn patted his cheeks with a little snow from the ice.

"Anderson — ?" began Mr. Sturgeon.

Pete's eyelids fluttered. "Hello, sir. Is it morning already?"

"Attaboy, Anderson!" approved Coach Flynn. "Way to shake it off!" He held up two fingers. "How many fingers do you see?"

Pete frowned. "Is this a trick question?"

Flynn slapped him on the shoulder. "You're okay. Take your time getting up. Two minutes to play."

"*No* minutes to play for Anderson," said the Headmaster firmly. "Nurse Hildegarde is waiting for us in the infirmary."

"But sir," protested Flynn weakly. "We have no backup goalie!"

"And the Andersons have only one son," said Mr. Sturgeon. "Hockey is a secondary matter in this instance. If he has had his 'bell rung,' as you put it, we shall wait until the vibrations cease."

Flynn nodded reluctantly, hope dying, and turned to the referee. "We'll need a few minutes," he said. "We have to dress another goalie."

"Who do you want in net?" Bruno asked the coach.

Flynn held his head. "We need everybody we've got up front. Hey — what about Fred?"

The answers came from everyone, and no two were alike:

"He's busy."

"He's sick."

"His aunt is sick."

"Fred who?"

"He's dead."

"He moved to Europe."

Boots's was the answer that got through. "Fred can't make it, sir. It'll have to be one of us."

"That's what you think!" said Wilbur in a strangled whisper. "Look!" He pointed to the stands behind the Macdonald Hall bench. Jordie Jones was gone.

"Oh, no," moaned Boots.

Flynn was agonizing over his decision. "Walton, you're pretty good in goal — no, we need you out here. Rampulsky — no. What am I — crazy? Hackenschleimer, you take up the most space — " He was interrupted by a roar from the crowd. A fully dressed Macdonald Hall goalie had stepped out of the dressing room and was making his way to the rink.

The coach's face lit up. "It's Fred!"

* * *

"I keep telling you," said Seth Dinkman in exasperation, "Jordie's at the game."

Goose Golden had just interrupted *Academy Blues* for the fourth time to ask after his client's whereabouts. "When's he coming back?"

"When the game is over, I guess. How should I know?"

Golden was sulky. "What does a California kid need to watch hockey for? It's cold in there. He could get a chill. Or pneumonia. It's crowded. He could get kidnapped!"

"Or — horror of horrors — he might have fun!" snapped the director. He waved his megaphone in Golden's face. "Now get out of here, or I'll shove this thing so far up your nose, every time you sneeze they'll hear it in Mexico City!"

Mumbling under his breath, Golden walked off the set. Sure, he knew he overprotected J.J. Who could blame him? A young kid in a dog-eat-dog adult world needed all the protection he could get.

On the other hand, Seth was right. This was no longer the three-year-old who had achieved fame and fortune as Cutesy Newbar. This was a young man who needed freedom, friends and excitement. He would let go. And in the meanwhile, he would drop by the arena — not to ride herd on J.J., of course. That would be unthinkable. This was Canada, and hockey was the national sport. He owed it to himself to soak up some of the local culture.

* * *

From the first whistle, York Academy unleashed a devastating barrage at the new goalie. They had 1:57 to send this game into overtime. If they didn't score, they would end their best season ever with a humiliating loss to the weakest Macs team in years. The Macdonald Hall defenders scrambled like chickens with their heads cut off in a vain attempt to clear the puck, but the attack was just too strong. The Cougars turned the Macdonald Hall hockey stadium into a shooting gallery, with Jordie Jones as the target.

His catching glove was just a blur, and he scrambled all over the crease, facing every shooter, stopping every bullet. He flopped, gloved, blocked and cleared with very little help from his defenders, who were being outplayed at every turn.

The Cougars' captain snared the puck and made a neat centring pass in front of the net. There was a wild shoving match as six players tried to bat at it, until Jordie reached out with his glove and closed it over the puck. The whistle blew. Thirty-two seconds remained on the clock.

The York captain was gasping. "That's your *backup* goalie? Who's the third-string — Martin Brodeur?"

"Bench strength," said Bruno proudly. To Boots he whispered, "Where'd Cutesy learn to play like that?"

"They've only got *good* shooters!" Boots rasped in an undertone. "They're going high, and Jordie's got a great glove! If anyone ever puts a dribbler along the ice, we're dead!"

On the very next face-off, Boots's fears came true. The York right winger tried a slap shot and partially missed, just topping the puck with the heel of his stick. A slow, lazy shot came gliding toward the net. Jordie moved out to meet it, his stick planted firmly on the top of his skates instead of flat on the ice.

Bruno and Boots both saw it at the same time. *"Your stick!"*

The puck slid lazily under the stick and between Jordie's feet toward the goal line.

"No-o-o-o!" howled Coach Flynn in horror.

Jordie wheeled, unable to see the puck, and as he turned his skate blade deflected it at the net. For one moment of exquisite agony, it looked as though the Macs' goalie himself would score the tying point for York Academy. But the shot hit the goalpost, flipped up and rolled away into the corner. There was an audible gasp of relief from the crowd.

Completely forgetting his position, Jordie abandoned the net and scrambled madly after the puck. Three Cougars roared in after him, meeting with an enormous crunch against the boards. The force of the collision sent the netminder's mask flying into the second row of seats. Three thousand pairs of eyes stared at the famous face playing goal for Macdonald Hall.

"Jordie Jones!" chorused the spectators, almost in perfect unison.

"Where?" In the fourteenth row, Goose Golden sat, polishing his glasses. He squinted at the ice, but it was just a blur. Slipping them onto his nose, he focused on a scene out of his wildest nightmares. J.J., at the centre of a pileup, surrounded by big burly boys armed with sticks and sharp blades. He leapt to his feet and opened his mouth to scream, but the wind left him as though he had been punched full-force in the stomach by the heavyweight champion of the world.

On the ice, the mad scrap for the puck continued as the seconds ticked away. The Macs dug furiously, but it was the York captain whose strength and skill prevailed. He pulled the puck loose and passed it back to the right defenceman, the hardest and most accurate shooter on the team.

Digging in the corner for something that was no longer there, it hit Jordie like ten tons of bricks — if he was here, who was in goal? *The net was empty!*

With a cry like Tarzan swinging through the trees, the actor took off for his net just as the Cougar defenceman wound up for a booming slap shot. Jordie didn't skate, but sprinted, to his post, digging his blades into the ice. From the point, a blistering drive was airborne, hurtling for the net. Jordie knew he wouldn't make it. He was going to cost Macdonald Hall this game. He left his feet in one final desperate leap to interpose himself between the puck and the net. Headfirst he dove, all his energy concentrating on this one action.

The lightning shot sizzled in on goal just as Jordie made his dive. The race was a tie. The puck hit Jordie right over the left eye and deflected harmlessly into the corner. Jordie landed in a heap on the ice.

The clock ticked down — 3–2–1 — a siren signalled the end of the game.

No one cheered. No one moved. All attention was on the fallen movie star.

At last, Jordie turned over with a groan. He cast his eye, already red and swelling, on the scoreboard and the expired clock, and raised his stick in ecstatic triumph.

Pandemonium broke loose.

Chapter 9

Meet the Press

Bruno and Boots got special permission to ride with Coach Flynn to York County Hospital that evening to visit the hero of the day.

They found him sitting up in bed, spirits high, watching himself in an old *Cutesy Newbar* rerun on TV. His eye was swollen shut, and the left side of his face was puffed out and purple, but the post-game grin was still there, and it stretched from ear to ear.

"I got in trouble," he said cheerfully. "Makeup says they can't make my face look normal for another ten days. Seth hit the ceiling."

"Join the club," said Boots. "The whole team is alternating on dishwashing duty."

Coach Flynn tried to look grim. "I think I might be in trouble, too. It's my business to know who my goalie is. I can never condone breaking the rules." He smiled all over his face. "But today I came very close."

"Too bad we got disqualified," said Jordie.

Bruno snorted. "Ineligible player — big deal. We all know who won. Who cares about the official story? And you were great,

Cutesy," he added with emphasis. "You were better than great. The team is flipping out over the game and what you did for us."

"Pete's all mad because he missed it," put in Boots.

"Is he okay?" Jordie inquired.

"Sure, fine," said Bruno. "We were kind of worried for a while, but then he asked if you and Fred were related — so we knew he was back to normal."

"You know, I'm fine, too, except for my eye," said Jordie, fidgeting restlessly. "I don't see why I have to stay here over-night."

Bruno surveyed the semiprivate room critically. "Hey, Cutesy, if you're such a big star, how come you have to share a room with somebody else?"

As if on cue, a hand reached out and pulled open the curtain that divided the room. There in the other bed lay Goose Golden, pale-faced and prostrated, a shattered man apparently breathing his last.

Mr. Flynn was horrified. "What happened?"

Golden glared at him balefully. "You!" he barely whispered. "A teacher, an educator, a respected man! Involving innocent children in a bloodbath! Barbarian! Savage! Philistine!"

"He's okay," supplied Jordie. "He got a little upset at the game today."

"Game?!" the manager spat. "I don't remember any game. Butchery. Atrocity. Mayhem. And in the middle of it — *my client*! I'm lucky to be alive!"

Jordie laughed. "*I'm* the guy with the black eye."

"It's my job to suffer for you," said Golden stubbornly.

"You should have seen him a couple of hours ago," Jordie

told the visitors. "He tried to get the doctor to put him on life support."

"He's a quack," muttered Golden. "What does he know about sickness?"

"It really is my fault," confessed Mr. Flynn. "Hockey is a great sport, but it *can* get a little rough."

"There were so many guys out there," raved Golden. "Did anything happen to them? No! It had to be *my client* who got hit right in the face with the ball!"

"It's a puck," corrected Bruno.

"It's a lethal weapon!" roared Golden, his strength returning. "It should be controlled by the government!"

At that moment, a white-coated doctor entered, accompanied by Seth Dinkman.

"The boy is fine," the doctor was saying. "There's no damage, not even a cut."

"But isn't there something you can give him to get that swelling down?" pleaded the director. "Money is no object."

The doctor smiled. "Money won't help. The swelling will reduce with time — no charge."

Dinkman made a face. "Money we have; time we don't. I've got a whole crew standing by. Our schedule is shot."

The doctor reached down and made a notation on Jordie's chart. "Sorry. He can check out first thing in the morning."

Dinkman looked dejected. "Well, how about the idiot, then?" he persisted, pointing at Golden. "Is he going to croak in the next five minutes, or what? If he is, I can stick around to say good-bye. Otherwise, I've got important things to do, like clipping my toenails."

"Come on, Seth," said Jordie with a grimace.

"It's a difficult diagnosis to make," the doctor explained. "There is nothing physically wrong with Mr. Golden. My best guess is that he had an instantaneous nervous breakdown at the rink today. All the stages that normally take months to evolve hit him in the span of three or four seconds. His recovery was just as fast. He can leave anytime."

Bruno pointed at the TV screen and let out a whoop. "Hey, Cutesy, there goes your diaper!"

Dinkman stared at Bruno. "What are *you* doing here?" He turned to Jordie. "What is *he* doing here?"

"I remember when we filmed this episode," Golden reminisced. "J.J. had diaper rash. Oh, how I suffered!"

"Well, boys," said Coach Flynn, "we'd better get going if we're going to be back at the Hall before lights-out. Goodnight, Jordie." He looked embarrassed. "And thanks for a terrific game."

The young man who had travelled the world, dined with presidents and starred with legends flashed him a lopsided grin. "This has been the greatest day of my life!"

* * *

"I don't care what Mr. Dinkman said," soothed Mrs. Sturgeon over Sunday breakfast. "It's not your fault."

The Headmaster stared morosely into his coffee. "It was I who suggested they let Jones live a little. And what was the result? It practically killed him."

"Oh, William, how many black eyes have we seen in our years at Macdonald Hall?"

"Hundreds," he replied. "Thousands. But none of them had

millions of dollars worth of equipment and man-hours waiting on their recovery."

"Mr. Dinkman is just a very excitable person," she explained. "I'm sure he didn't mean all those terrible things he said."

He smiled wryly. "You mean about how Macdonald Hall is an insane asylum, and I am the head inmate?"

"You have to understand," she persisted. "He'd just had a very nasty shock. But today his stuntmen will arrive, and he'll be able to shoot all the scenes without Jordie, and I'm sure it will turn out that he hasn't lost very much time after all." She smiled wider. "And we *did* beat York Academy — sort of."

It was the one comment that could lighten the Headmaster's mood. "I thought Hartley was going to have a seizure," he said with relish. "It will always be one of the great pleasures of my life that I was able to return to the rink in time to see the look on his face." He sighed heavily. "I suppose the worst is over. Dinkman has invited reporters to keep the Jones boy occupied so he can't get into any more mischief during his recovery. And on Tuesday, Walton and his crowd are off on the wilderness survival trip. By the time they return, the movie people will have left for California."

"You see?" his wife said triumphantly. "It's all working out beautifully."

The Headmaster buttered his toast. "It is always in the home stretch that the racehorse stumbles, Mildred. My instincts tell me that the Jones boy and Walton and O'Neal are an explosive combination. As for Dinkman — perhaps you'd better make him some more of your kiwi flan. It seems to have a soothing effect on him."

But not even kiwi flan did Seth Dinkman's temper any good. The director was on the warpath. The arrival of his stuntmen, and the satisfaction of putting his idle crew to work, calmed him slightly, but the smallest equipment failure or human error had him in an instant rage. And the mere sight of Jordie and his swollen eye reduced him to screaming hysterics.

On Sunday morning, when Bruno approached the director to beg for one more chance at an extra's job, Dinkman ordered six burly security men to take him out and execute him.

"Aw, come on, boss," said the leader. "We can't do that."

"Are you telling me I can't execute whoever I want?" Dinkman shrieked. "I'm the *director*!"

The guards gently led Bruno a safe distance away. "Look, kid," advised the leader. "You've got a lot of moxie. But Seth is pretty uptight right now, so don't bug him, okay? Maybe you'll get a chance to be in another movie someday."

The director had decided that if Jordie Jones wasn't going to earn his money by acting, he was going to be put to work promoting *Academy Blues*. He sent out a press release, stating that the young star had suffered a grievous injury in a hockey game that he had single-handedly won. Reporters came flocking like ants to a picnic. They jammed all the hotels in neighbouring towns and swarmed all over the campus, waving press papers, cameras, microphones and notepads. From nine in the morning to nine at night, Jordie told his story over and over to representatives of everything from the *Biloxi Post-Dispatch* to *World News Tonight*, and from *Sports Illustrated* to the *Columbia Journal of Medicine*.

Goose Golden was at his side every waking moment. Jordie Jones was virtually a prisoner.

* * *

Precisely at 6 PM, Headmaster Sturgeon closed up his office and started home for dinner. He had spent most of the afternoon writing a report of the hockey incident for Macdonald Hall's Board of Directors and was annoyed at having wasted a Sunday on nonsense.

As he made his way along the Faculty Building's main corridor, he came across the crew of a TV news mobile unit about to enter the music room.

"Excuse me, gentlemen," he said, hurrying over. "You must be in the wrong place. This is a school building and off-limits to the media."

"Oh, it's okay," said the cameraman. "We're here for the press conference."

"I'm afraid you are mistaken," said the Headmaster. "There is no press conference here."

"Yeah, nobody seems to know about it," put in the reporter disgustedly. "You guys sure aren't very organized. You'd better talk to your boss, this guy — uh" — he consulted a notebook — "Walton. He set the whole thing up."

There was a pause, then "*Bruno* Walton?"

"Yeah, that's the guy. Real big-time operator. He got all the hockey players together to release their statements."

Mr. Sturgeon opened the door to the music room. An amazing sight met his eyes. The room was jam-packed with media people and brilliant with floodlights. All cameras, microphones and eyes were directed to the front. Several long tables were pushed together, and behind them sat the sixteen Macdonald Hall Macs, preparing for their hour of fame.

Bruno stood at the centre, leaning on a small portable podium. He flashed a thumbs-up signal to Mark, who was filming from the first row of reporters.

"Ladies and gentlemen of the press," he announced pompously. Then, in a more natural tone, "Thanks for coming. I'm Bruno Walton, and I play left defence, so I was right there on the ice when Cutesy got nailed in the face with that puck. But enough about me. Now we can take your questions, starting with this guy here — yeah, you from *The New York Times*."

A quiet, icy voice from the doorway spoke before the *Times* reporter had a chance to open his mouth. "You will go to your rooms and remain there until further notice."

The seated members of the team scattered through the ranks of the media toward the door, Mark hot on their heels. Alone at the front, Bruno stammered, "Uh — the press conference is officially postponed on account of — uh — I gotta go!" Abandoning the podium, he darted after his teammates.

A confused murmur rippled through the crowd.

"Hey," came a voice, "how can it be over when it hasn't started yet?"

"Maybe it's a coffee break."

Mr. Sturgeon addressed the assembled media, softly but clearly. "Ladies and gentlemen, I regret that your time has been wasted. There will be no statements made here. You will restrict your activities to the movie set on the east lawn. Good day."

At the door, Bruno was attempting to slip nonchalantly past

the Headmaster when an iron grip on his shoulder stopped him cold.

"Let go, sir. I have to report to my room."

Mr. Sturgeon glared down at him. "I require a word with you."

Bruno nodded. "I was afraid of that, sir."

They supervised the evacuation of the music room, with the Headmaster fielding the many questions and complaints from the disgruntled reporters. Then he turned and fixed Bruno with a fishy stare.

"I don't know what you think you're running here, Walton, but *I* am running a school. And I *will* be obeyed. Is that clear?"

"Yes, sir."

"You have been involved in a great deal of mischief before, but never have you been so out of control. Do you realize that, were you not going on the wilderness survival trip, I would probably be forced to suspend you, just to get you away from here for a while?"

Bruno cleared his throat carefully. "This may not be the right time to mention it, sir, but I've been meaning to ask you if I could maybe — you know — kind of not go on the trip."

Mr. Sturgeon shook his head in disbelief. "This is exactly my point. You are not listening to me. I stand here talking about suspension, and you are already embarking on your next escapade."

"Well, sir," said Bruno, "you know how you always say we have to keep up with our studies. I'm just starting to get really into my courses this term — "

"Try again, Walton."

"Well, I had this great story about being allergic to bears — "

Mr. Sturgeon smiled grimly. "And where did you discover this allergy? The zoo?"

"The circus," said Bruno, inventing rapidly.

"Then perhaps you are only allergic to dancing bears," said the Headmaster. "Or bears that walk tightropes, or ride tricycles. Walton, I know why you want to stay behind. You still have the grossly mistaken idea that you are going to get yourself into that confounded movie. It is a fever that has taken you over, and I expect you to go on that trip and come back cured."

Bruno sighed. "That's not exactly true, sir. I would have been satisfied with just getting on TV, but you wouldn't let me have a press conference."

"Indeed I would not," said the Headmaster emphatically. "Do you realize the embarrassment you might have caused this institution before a worldwide audience?" He gazed down the empty hall and frowned in annoyance. "O'Neal, come out from behind that door."

The white face of Boots O'Neal appeared, and the boy himself stepped out into the open.

"This whole miserable business has had its amusing aspects," said Mr. Sturgeon, "and that has saved you more than once, Walton. But now I am not feeling indulgent, and, if you will notice, I am not smiling. Neither will you smile if I catch you anywhere near the east lawn again. And now I am going for my dinner, and I suggest you do the same."

"Uh — sir," called Bruno as the Headmaster marched toward the exit.

"Bruno — shhh!" whispered Boots.

Mr. Sturgeon wheeled and fixed Bruno with blazing eyes. "This had better be good!"

Bruno flushed. "Well, it's just that you sent the team to their rooms until further notice, and it's dinner time, and if you're going home — well, you know Wilbur — "

In his anger Mr. Sturgeon had completely forgotten the team. "I was coming to that. Tell them they may leave their rooms."

He stormed out of the building.

Bruno exhaled deeply. "First Dinkman, then Golden, now The Fish. People are going to have to lighten up around here if I'm ever going to get into that movie."

Boots stared at him. "You know, Bruno, we have a great time at the Hall. We break a few rules and play practical jokes and we're not goody-goodies who do everything we're told. But we both know that when The Fish starts using words like 'suspend,' it's time to lay off. Because the fun stops if we're not at Macdonald Hall anymore, right?"

Bruno shrugged it off. "Don't worry. The Fish was just kind of steamed — "

"No!" his roommate interrupted. "Look, you've had your shot, but now it's too risky. If you won't listen to The Fish, listen to me. Don't get yourself suspended or expelled. *Chill out!*"

Chapter 10

The Stuntman

The first wave of Jordie Jones interviews hit the papers, radio and television on Sunday night, and by Monday morning, the actor's trailer looked like a florist's shop. Movie security had been up all night chasing off Miss Scrimmage's girls, who streamed across the road, singly and in packs, with get-well flowers for their hero. These were mostly tulips, daffodils, crocuses and snowdrops filched from the school's spring flower beds. There were also potted African violets from indoor windowsills, ferns and parlour palms from Miss Scrimmage's sitting room and the entire prize cactus garden from the Headmistress's conservatory. Those who could not come up with any flowers made artificial ones out of pipe cleaners and Kleenex. This entitled them to sign the giant *Get Well, Jordie* card, which also arrived during the night, and bore over three hundred signatures.

The news reached Mr. Sturgeon when Miss Scrimmage stormed his doorstep at 6:30 AM.

"This is all your fault!" she shrilled. "Now you'll see why I need my shotgun to protect my poor innocent girls! My school was robbed last night!"

The Headmaster was shocked. "What was taken?" he asked, tying his bathrobe and stepping out onto the porch. "Money? Jewellery?"

"Flowers!" she cried. "The outdoor beds are picked clean! It looks like the great hurricane of 'thirty-one! And all my plants! Even my famous award-winning cactus garden!"

Mr. Sturgeon turned to his wife, who had appeared in the doorway. "Mildred, tie down the geranium. There are plant bandits about."

Miss Scrimmage was outraged. "You mock me, sir! But do you deny that my girls were in danger?"

"I do indeed." The Headmaster yawned. He pointed toward the east lawn. Even at a distance it was obvious that Jordie Jones's trailer was festooned with flowers and greenery.

"Humph!" snorted Miss Scrimmage. "How disgraceful! A wealthy young man like that should be buying his own flowers!" And she stormed off, muttering something about filing more lawsuits.

The next reaction to the floral tribute came from Goose Golden. At quarter past seven, he wandered out of his trailer without his glasses. Since Miss Scrimmage's prize-winning cacti and some of the larger ferns were as high as three metres tall, he saw only a blur of green where Jordie's trailer was supposed to be. In a panic, he decided that the camper and his client had been towed away during the night. Howling, he ran forward, tearing his white pyjamas and scratching his hands and face on the cactus needles, which also lifted the toupee clean off his head. In his distress, he surged forward, running headfirst into the trailer door.

It was the first time anyone had seen Seth Dinkman laugh since Jordie Jones's hockey debut.

* * *

All the commotion went unnoticed in Dormitory 3, where Bruno and Boots were laying out gear for their wilderness survival trip. They had the day off classes to make sure they had exactly the right equipment and supplies and to get plenty of rest for tomorrow's 5 AM departure.

"Let's see," said Boots, checking the things spread out on his bed. "Sleeping bag, underwear, socks, boots, flannel shirts, jacket, three pairs of jeans, long johns and raincoat." He put a toothbrush, toothpaste and a comb into a plastic bag and tossed it onto the pile. "I think that's everything."

Bruno was sitting on the edge of his bed, arms folded, sulking. In his open duffel was exactly one item — bug spray.

"Bruno, there aren't going to be any bugs this early in the year."

Bruno didn't look up. "There are always bugs. Who else would be stupid enough to go on this trip? Us and bugs."

Boots took out his own bag and began jamming his clothes inside. "Hurry up. Mr. Fudge'll be by any second to check our stuff."

His roommate didn't seem to hear him. "I can't believe The Fish ordered me to stay away from the movie — just like that! Where am I ever going to get another chance to be in a movie?"

"Why pin it on The Fish?" said Boots. "For him, he's been great about this. Blame Dinkman and, mostly, blame yourself. Think of all those second chances Jordie got for you. You goobered up every one of them. Now, why don't you just chalk it up to experience and forget it?"

"That's easy for you to say," said Bruno. "You're in the movie, tossing around some stupid baseball while Cutesy walks from point A to point B. So are Larry, Wilbur, Pete — even Sidney finally made it to a crowd scene. *Everybody's* in that idiotic movie. I mean, do I have the plague or something?"

At that moment, there was a knock on the door, and Boots admitted Mr. Fudge.

"Now, let's see how we're doing," the Housemaster said briskly, examining Boots's duffel. "Yes. Excellent, O'Neal. A very efficient job of packing. And how's Walton coming along?" He turned his attention to the bag with the bug spray. "Hmmm. Travelling light, I see."

"Sorry, sir," mumbled Bruno. "I'm having a little trouble getting my act together today."

"Here are your kits." Mr. Fudge placed two canvas drawstring bags on the floor at the door. "Speed it up, Walton. Just follow O'Neal's example. And make sure you don't forget anything. Survival in the bush is eighty percent planning and preparation." And he marched out to check on the other campers.

"I wonder what the other twenty percent is," mused Bruno darkly. "Outrunning the cannibals?"

"Bruno, we're going to a provincial park! There aren't going to be any cannibals — except maybe Wilbur if the food runs low." He opened up his kit and dumped its contents on the bed beside his bag. Out spilled a tin mess kit, a coil of rope, a small bottle of alcohol, gauze bandages and a Swiss Army knife.

Bruno stared at the pocketknife. "Good thing Sidney's not coming. We'd be sliced to bits on the bus."

Boots had to laugh. "Just hurry up and pack."

In the room Wilbur and Larry shared in Dormitory 2, Coach Flynn stood, arms folded, as Wilbur removed jar after jar of peanut butter from his luggage.

"Couldn't I just keep *one*?" whined the big boy.

Flynn laughed. "This is a survival trip, Hackenschleimer. We take along minimal rations and forage for the rest."

"Forage?! If you think I'm going to eat a chipmunk — !"

Larry butted in, almost hysterical. "He means berries and roots and nuts and stuff. Take it easy. You can live for five days without peanut butter."

Wilbur said nothing, but his expression clearly indicated that he didn't think so.

Down the hall in room 201, Elmer Drimsdale was excitedly preparing for a comprehensive nature study. He was busily filling his backpack with spiral notebooks for observations and small containers for specimens. For the next five days, no leaf would go unsketched, no soil would go unsampled, no wildlife unstudied in all of huge Algonquin Park.

Like Bruno and Wilbur, Mark Davies also had reservations about the trip.

"I can't go," he told Sidney, his roommate, for the umpteenth time. "What about my documentary? I'll miss all the stunts!"

Sidney shrugged. "Don't tell me. Tell The Fish."

"I already did. He said no one gets out of Die-in-the-Woods."

"Well, don't let it spoil the trip for you," counselled Sidney. "When I went, we had a lot of fun."

Mark stared at him. "You mean to tell me you went for a five-day trip without busting the whole thing up?"

"Of course," said Sidney defiantly. He looked thoughtful. "Well, there *was* that one time — " He frowned. "— and then I — yeah, and — " He shrugged at Mark. "Okay, I did six clumsy things. That's not so bad."

"Not for you," his roommate agreed. He hefted his video camera. "I guess I'll get in my last filming. I hope there's something good going on."

* * *

"I can't believe you still haven't even started packing," said Boots as he and Bruno strolled through the greenery at the northern fringe of the campus.

"That'll take two seconds. I can do it anytime," Bruno replied lethargically.

"Bruno, if you think just because you're not packed you won't have to go on the trip, you can forget it!"

"It's not that," said Bruno. "Now that I know I'm not going to be in *Academy Blues*, I can't get up very much energy for anything, let alone Die-in-the-Woods."

"Hey, look," said Boots, pointing towards the east lawn, where the three-metre-high model of the Faculty Building now sat, finished.

"I can't look at that thing anymore," said Bruno. "I keep expecting a miniature Fish to come out the door and put me to work washing very small dishes."

"I guess we won't be here to see them blow it up, or burn it down, or whatever," commented Boots.

Bruno sighed. "You want to know what the worst part is? Cutesy hasn't even come to see us, after all we've done for him!"

"Like putting him in the hospital?"

"Like assisting in his social development," Bruno amended. "We gave a poker night in honour of his birthday, we brought him to a dance, we let him join our hockey team — we adopted him, Boots! And where is he now? He knows we're going away tomorrow and he'll be gone when we get back. I think we deserve at least a good-bye."

Boots nodded. "I can't figure that out, either. Maybe he's planning to come by sometime tonight."

"Maybe," said Bruno dubiously. "But I'm not holding my breath."

"Hey," Boots pointed up the path ahead of them. "Isn't that Jordie over there?"

The two hurried to the top of the grassy knoll to join the blond figure poised on a racing bike. Just as Bruno was about to hail the actor, one of Seth Dinkman's production assistants ran up the hill. "Relax," he called to the rider. "Camera three's acting up. It'll be twenty minutes, minimum."

The figure dismounted and removed his jacket and a blond wig, and Bruno and Boots could see that he was not Jordie, but a short, slight, dark-haired man in his early twenties.

Galvanized with excitement, Bruno grabbed Boots and hauled him into the bushes.

"What's the big idea?" Boots complained.

"Shhh!" Bruno hissed. "That guy — he's a double for Cutesy! That's why he's wearing the wig!"

They fell silent. Bored and restless, the man began to explore his surroundings. Whistling nervously through his teeth, he wandered by them on the path.

Bruno waited until he had gone, then dragged Boots over to the bicycle. Flopping to the ground, he crawled forward and peered over the top of the hill. At the bottom was the *Academy Blues* crew, camera lenses directed towards the path down. "See that?" he whispered. "They're going to film this guy, posing as Cutesy, riding down that path." His eyes sparkled. "Only it isn't going to be him. It's going to be me."

Boots was horrified. "Are you crazy? You promised The Fish no more sneaking into the movie!"

"Not exactly," grinned Bruno. "He said he didn't want to catch me anywhere near the east lawn. Well, this isn't east. It's north."

"It's north *and* east," said Boots.

"Look," said Bruno, "no one's going to catch me. The reason they can use a double for this scene is because it's a long shot. All you can see is the wig and the jacket. It can be me just as easily as that guy." He scrambled into the jacket and clapped the wig on his head. "See?"

"Well, what about the guy, then?" Boots challenged. "You think he's going to let you do his job?"

"That's where you come in," Bruno explained reasonably.

"Me?!"

"Go find him," Bruno instructed, "and tell him the scene's been delayed another half hour. Then engage him in conversation to make sure he doesn't come back here. Simple."

"I won't do it!" said Boots stubbornly. "I'm not helping you get suspended!"

Bruno looked hurt. "Well, that's just great. First Cutesy spits in my eye and now my best friend. All I ever wanted to do was be in the movie. But no. Melvin can't put himself out for me."

"Aw, come on, Bruno — "

"Well, at least now I've learned my lesson," Bruno continued dramatically. "Friendship isn't a true thing. It's just something you have until it becomes inconvenient. Then you throw it away like garbage, old shoes, apple cores, the two of clubs — "

"Oh, all right!" cried Boots. "I'll do it! But when we get expelled, you have to explain it to my folks."

Bruno awarded him a hearty slap on the shoulder. "You'll see! It'll be great! Now get going!"

Boots jogged off in search of the Jordie Jones stand-in. He found the man along the same path, just around a corner, sitting in a small grove of pine trees, munching on a chocolate bar.

"Hi," said Boots. "Mr. Dinkman sent me with a message."

"Yeah, yeah. More trouble with camera three, right?"

"Right," said Boots, pleased to have the story made up for him.

"Let me guess — another thirty minutes?"

"At least," confirmed Boots.

"It figures," the man muttered. "They call me at midnight L.A. time, throw me on the red-eye to Toronto — five hours in the air — rush me up here and sit me on top of a mountain to wait."

Boots smiled lamely. "That's show business."

"Tell me about it!" said the man. "The stars — they get treated like royalty. Nobody makes them wait. But we stunt-men — forget it!"

Boots goggled. "You're a *stuntman*?"

The man nodded. "You're talking to the best, kid. A specialist. We're the guys they call when the regular stunt people chicken out." He broke his candy bar in two. "Want some Baby Ruth?"

But Boots was already running up the path, screaming, *"Bruno! Get off that bike! It's a stunt! Bruno!"* He roared around the corner just in time to hear a megaphone voice declare, *"Action!"* For a split second he could see Bruno atop the bicycle, poised at the edge of the incline. Then his roommate pushed off and dropped out of view.

"No! Come back! It's a *stunt*!"

Heart pounding, he ran to the crest of the hill and looked down. Bruno was rocketing down the path on the bicycle, the hair of his fine blond wig streaming out behind him, his feet on the pedals just a blur. He shot to the bottom of the hill and levelled off, streaking toward the film crew.

Boots frowned. That was the stunt that the regular people found too dangerous? They brought a guy all the way from California for *this*? To ride a bike down a hill? What was the big deal about — ?

BOOM!!!

The ground under Bruno's front wheel blew to pieces, sending dirt and grass flying in all directions. A geyser of water shot straight up with tremendous force, hurling bike and rider three metres in the air. At the highest point atop the pillar of water, Bruno let go of the handlebars and curled himself up into a ball. He hit the ground with an enormous splash, rolled and lay flat on his back, dazed. Water poured down on him.

"Cut! Perfect! Print it!" came Seth Dinkman's voice over the megaphone.

Boots was tearing down the path as fast as he could go without gravity taking him head over heels to the bottom. Out of the corner of his eye, he could see the real stuntman roaring over the crest of the hill, bellowing, "What happened? What was that noise?"

Boots kept on running, his eyes on his roommate's inert form. The stuntman would be furious, but all he could think of was that Bruno was probably dead.

"Shut off the water," ordered the director.

A technician turned a large valve, and the geyser petered out.

Dinkman jogged up to where Bruno lay. "Charlie, that was fantastic! I can't believe something finally went right!"

The entire crew gathered around the weary and waterlogged stuntman, including Mark Davies and his video camera.

Bruno sat up, and the wig fell off.

The director took one look at him and dropped his megaphone in the mud.

"Aaaaah!"

Chapter II

Nothing and Nowhere

"You mean after all that you're *still* not in *Academy Blues*?" Boots asked in disbelief.

Bruno sighed wearily. "It's a conspiracy. You can't be in a stunt unless you belong to the stuntmen's union. They should have told me that before they tried to blow me off the face of the earth."

"You're the one who made such a big deal about the scene where they were fixing the sewer pipe. You said, 'How can it be broken if it didn't break yet?' Well, today it broke."

"Yeah," said Bruno. "But nobody said it was going to break on me. Who would have thought one little grapefruit could do so much damage?"

"You've got no right to complain!" said Boots hotly. "You make your own problems. Mr. Dinkman didn't exactly hand-cuff you to that bike and push you down the hill, you know."

Bruno crawled into bed and pulled the covers up to his ears. "You've made your point, Boots. And let me tell you, I am *finished* with the movie business! I don't want anything to do with an industry where they take a guy and put him through what I went through today, stuntman or not. I've never been so scared in all my life!"

"Boy, was Mr. Dinkman ever mad!" said Boots.

"No kidding. He said it's going to cost eighty thousand dollars to reshoot that scene." Bruno sighed heavily. "At least he's not telling The Fish. That would be the finishing touch to this perfect day. I'd get on that bike again before I'd face The Fish over this."

"Lucky for us, so would Dinkman," Boots replied. "The Fish would kick the whole movie company out if he knew one of us got caught in a stunt, even if it *was* our fault." He climbed into bed and reached for the lamp. He paused. "I guess Jordie's not coming."

"Guess not," mumbled Bruno sleepily.

Boots hesitated. "Maybe we should go over there, and — you know — say good-bye."

"Not me," was Bruno's reply. "Cutesy knows where to find us. If he didn't come, it's because he wasn't interested."

"Yeah, but maybe with all the media people around he hasn't had a chance — "

"He's the big hotshot," said Bruno. "If he gets sick of doing interviews, he just has to say 'bug off.' Can we say that to our teachers when homework gets too heavy? Besides, if I get caught on the east lawn, I'm hamburger. Let Cutesy take some risks for a change."

"Why are you being so stubborn?" asked Boots. "At least *talk* to the guy."

Bruno rolled over, and at first Boots thought his roommate was asleep. But then Bruno's voice reached him.

"Call me stupid, call me old-fashioned, call me a wimp — friendship is not a two-week hobby. Not even for movie stars."

Boots switched off the light, frowning. "I've got this weird feeling we forgot to do something."

Bruno groaned. "Whatever it is, it can't be as important as me getting some rest. The sooner this lousy day ends, the better."

"Goodnight."

Bruno was already snoring.

* * *

They were awakened by an insistent banging at the door.

Bruno rolled over and opened one eye just a crack. It was pitch-dark. "Are you crazy?" he moaned plaintively. "It's the middle of the night!"

"It's four forty-five," came Mr. Fudge's voice. "Get up, Walton. We're leaving in fifteen minutes."

"The trip!" hissed Boots, darting to the bathroom and splashing cold water on his face.

"Oh, yeah, the trip," mumbled Bruno. "How could I forget about the — uh — uh — whatever it was — " He sat up and swung his legs over the side of his bed. That was as far as he got. His upper body slumped back to the mattress.

"Hurry up, Bruno!" coaxed Boots frantically, slipping into his clothes. He zipped his duffel shut and tossed it over his shoulder, tucking his sleeping bag under the strap.

"Yeah, yeah, yeah," murmured Bruno. He struggled to his feet and picked up his own luggage. "Hey, this is lighter than I thought." He looked inside. His duffel contained exactly one item — bug spray. "Oops," he declared mildly.

Boots stared at the near-empty bag. "Oh, no! *That's* what we forgot! You haven't packed yet!"

"Ten minutes," came the Housemaster's voice.

Bruno was awake now, barrelling around the room like a whirlwind, pulling clothes out of drawers and throwing them at the bag. Then came the packing stage, with Bruno stomping his wadded-up belongings inside the overstuffed duffel, while working the zipper with one hand and combing his hair with the splayed fingers of the other.

"Come on, Walton, O'Neal," called Mr. Fudge. "What's the problem? We're leaving in two minutes."

"Coming, sir," called Bruno, heaving his sleeping bag under his arm. "Well?" he said to his roommate. "You're holding up Die-in-the-Woods."

"You're in your pyjamas," Boots pointed out.

Finally Mr. Fudge loaded the last two campers onto the bus, and the wilderness survival trip started out more or less on time. In addition to Bruno and Boots, the party consisted of Wilbur, Larry, Pete, Mark, Elmer and Calvin Fihzgart. Mr. Fudge and Coach Flynn were the staff supervisors.

As they pulled down the drive to the highway, Boots looked out the window at the caravan of trailers on the east lawn. Usually the scene of so much bustling activity, it was quiet and dark. He had been hoping for one particular figure to break the peace with good-bye shouts and waves.

He sighed. "I guess it's early for Jordie to be up," he commented lamely.

Bruno was already ninety percent back to sleep, his eyes closed, his seat in full reclining position. "I've decided to sleep through Die-in-the-Woods, so I don't want to be disturbed by too much talking. And *any* talking about Cutesy Newbar is too much in my book."

Boots squinted into the pre-dawn gloom. "I can't figure out why he didn't even say good-bye."

"I can figure it out just fine," said Bruno. "These movie stars are all alike. They blow like the wind. One minute we're Cutesy's best friends in the world. The next — boom! We're lepers."

"He should have at least come to see us before the trip," Boots agreed reluctantly.

"I've had it with these Hollywood types," Bruno went on, warming to the subject. "First Dinkman, and now Cutesy. There's no friendship! There's no loyalty! 'Oh, we were best pals and lifelong chums? Too bad. I'll get someone else for my next movie.'"

"Don't you think you're overdoing it a little?" came a whisper from under the seat in front of them.

Boots stared, but the orator in Bruno was aroused, and there was no stopping him now.

"Overdoing it? Hah! You can't overdo it with a guy like Cutesy. I was right about him the first time. No wonder he got famous with his butt. It's the part that best symbolizes the whole person. Look how he turned Scrimmage's against us. He's nothing but a low-down, shallow, no-good, pretty-faced, mealy-mouthed — "

"— great guy," finished the whisper.

Boots grabbed Bruno by the hair and angled his head so that he was looking down at the floor. There, at their feet, lay Jordie

Jones, grinning and waving. The swelling in his black eye had gone down considerably. He now looked boyish rather than grotesque.

"Cutesy, what're you *doing* here?" croaked Bruno.

"Stowing away," the actor whispered back.

Bruno and Boots stared at him, then at each other.

"Seth has me scheduled with interviews twelve hours a day," Jordie explained, "and Goose is treating me like a criminal. I can't handle it any more."

Boots slapped his knee. "I *told* you that's why he didn't come to see us!"

"I tried to! I even climbed out the window of my trailer because Security was watching the door." He shuddered. "Goose was there. He didn't have his glasses on, so he thought I was kidnapping me."

Bruno laughed. "You're a real friend, Cutesy. I never doubted you for a minute."

Boots stared at him. "Just a second ago, he was a low-down — "

Bruno dismissed this. "I never think straight before sun-up. Hey, Cutesy, I hope you know what you're doing. You're going to be in some major hot water for taking off on *Academy Blues*."

"Kind of," agreed the star. "But Seth still won't be able to use me until my eye heals, and we've already shot most of my scenes. So he can't say I'm sabotaging the schedule."

Boots went suddenly white. "Forget *you*! What about *us*? When The Fish finds out you're on this trip, we'll never be able to convince him it wasn't our fault!"

"I'll explain that the whole thing was my idea and you were as surprised as anybody," offered the actor.

Boots shook his head. "He won't believe it! Not after all those other times! Bruno and I'll get expelled!"

Jordie looked dejected. "You're right. It's too risky for you guys. When we stop at a gas station, I'll sneak out and take a taxi back to the school."

"No way," said Bruno firmly. "You're *our friend*, and we'll never let you down. If you want to stow away on this trip, then that's the way it's going to happen, period."

Boots nodded, a little less certainly than Bruno.

Jordie grinned from ear to ear. "You guys are great!"

Boots was first to come back down to earth. "But how are we going to pull it off? The Coach and Mr. Fudge would recognize Jordie in a second. And even if we can keep his face hidden, they know we're only eight guys. If they count nine, it's game over!"

But Bruno's eyes were closing again. "Details, details," he murmured. "We've got three and a half hours to work that stuff out." He yawned hugely. "If we can get Cutesy up there and keep him hidden long enough for the bus to take off and leave us, we should be in great shape for our next move, which is — uh — " He drifted off into sleep.

Jordie looked up at Boots. "That's the only problem with Bruno," he whispered. "He's a bundle of nerves."

Boots was nervous enough for the three of them. He sat in stiff-necked misery, hardly daring to glance down at Jordie for fear one of the teachers would ask what he was looking at. He held his breath every time Coach Flynn or Mr. Fudge strolled up and down the centre aisle.

Jordie was completely unperturbed. He lay in a semi-crouch under the seat, humming along with the half-hearted choruses of "Ninety-nine Bottles of Beer on the Wall" that occasionally swelled among the sleepy occupants of the bus.

Mark Davies knelt on his seat, pointing his video camera out the open window, recording the scenery that whizzed by.

"How's this going to fit into your idiot documentary?" grumbled Wilbur, still in a bad mood over having to leave his peanut butter at home.

"This is for my next documentary," Mark explained. "A travelogue on Die-in-the-Woods."

"This trip is right up my alley!" crowed Calvin Fihzgart. "Living off the land, struggling against the elements, chopping down trees, eating what you kill — "

"I'd like to kill a jar of peanut butter right about now," said Wilbur mournfully.

"I guess you've done a lot of camping," commented Pete to Calvin.

"This is my first time, but I'm going to be great!" At 8 AM, the bus pulled into a roadside diner, and the boys filed in for their last meal in civilization. Jordie waited until passengers and driver had gone into the truck stop before clambering out of his hiding place. He treated himself to a trip to the bathroom and stepped into the phone booth outside the building. Much dialling later, he was talking to his parents' answering machine in California.

"Hi, Mom and Dad, it's me. I'm taking off on my own for a few days, so don't worry. And if Goose and Seth call, tell them just to sit tight. I'll be back. 'Bye."

Inside, Calvin was staring distastefully at the large stack of pancakes on the plate in front of him. "What's the matter, Fihzgart?" called Coach Flynn, his mouth full. "Aren't you hungry?"

"I can't eat this," said Calvin reasonably. "I didn't kill it."

Bruno leaned over and plunged his knife deep into Calvin's breakfast. "There," he said. "It's dead now."

"Walton!" snapped Mr. Fudge. "Keep your knife to yourself. And take those pancakes out of your pocket. Do you think I'm blind?"

"There goes Jordie's breakfast," whispered Boots.

"Pass the word," Bruno murmured, unfolding lint-covered pancakes and placing them back on the dish. "Every guy sneaks one thing back for Cutesy."

By nine-thirty, they passed through the main town of Algonquin Park and, half an hour later, left the highway for a dirt road that led into the bush. For the next twenty minutes they bumped along, until, abruptly, the road ended.

"Okay," called Mr. Flynn cheerfully. "Everybody out. We're here."

Bruno looked out the window and then at the coach. "You're kidding."

But by that time Calvin Fihzgart was already at the bus door, scratching to get out.

The boys made sure to crowd around Jordie, keeping him hidden as they filed reluctantly off the bus. But the two teachers were far too preoccupied with the unloading of the gear to notice that they had acquired an extra boy.

"All right," said the driver once the passengers and their

equipment were standing in the scrub and weeds. "I'll be here to pick you up in five days. Uh — have a good time."

"Very funny," muttered Wilbur under his breath. Mark filmed the bus as it turned around, drove off and disappeared in the distance.

Next came the hiking stage. This was three solid hours straight into the woods, weighted down with packs, tents, supplies and the school canoe, a wood-and-birchbark replica of the kind used by fur traders in pioneer times. Bruno and Boots called it the S.S. *Drown-in-the-Woods*. Since the craft was carried portage-style on the shoulders of two boys, Jordie was quick to be one of them. That enabled him to keep his face hidden for the whole trek.

"Not bad," he whispered back to Wilbur, who was bringing up the rear.

Wilbur glared down at the pine needles underfoot. "Movie star or not, anybody who goes on Die-in-the-Woods on *purpose* is an idiot!"

It was rough going. There was no path, so everyone followed Coach Flynn, who was navigating by compass and recording their movements in a small spiral notebook. Each step was made more difficult by slippery, muddy ground, brought on by recent rain and spring melting. They snaked their way through the underbrush, which grew more dense as they penetrated the forest. Branches scratched at their hands and faces, and patchy sunlight dappled the ground.

To make matters worse, the botany lecture from Elmer Drimsdale began with the first tree and never let up for a second.

"Ah, the common Norway spruce, *Picea abies*. I recognize

the long, spreading branches. And this is *Acer saccharum*, the sugar maple." He frowned. "It looks a little stunted. I'll have to take a bark sample to do a proper acid rain analysis."

"You do that," yawned Larry, struggling under the huge backpack full of canned goods he and Pete were carrying.

They stopped in a small clearing in the thick bush, a damp and chilly place, and Coach Flynn announced that this was the perfect spot. To the boys, it looked like every other spot they'd seen in the last few kilometres, except that down a sharp rocky slope they could see a sparkling blue lake through the heavy vegetation.

"Okay," instructed the coach. "Our first priorities are drinking water and shelter." He pointed at the lake. "We've got water. Now we break out the tents."

As the boys unstrapped the tent kits, Mr. Fudge sidled up to the coach. "Alex, I just counted the kids. I think we've got a problem."

Flynn was horrified. "*What*? We *lost* somebody?"

The Housemaster put his face right up to the coach's ear and whispered, "We *gained* somebody."

Coach Flynn cast his eyes around the clearing. ". . . six, seven, eight — nine. How come we have nine?"

"Interest?" added Bruno hopefully.

Boots breathed deeply. He had known this moment would come, but even so, it was painful to watch.

Mr. Flynn scanned a few faces, then roared over to the edge of the clearing where Wilbur and Jordie were trying to look inconspicuous. Guided by Larry and Pete, they edged along the slope that led down to the water.

"Hackenschleimer, put down that canoe!"

With twin sighs, the bearers lowered their burden to the ground, revealing two faces — the wry embarrassment of Wilbur Hackenschleimer and the famous blue eyes of Jordie Jones. In resignation, Larry and Pete tossed the enormous grocery parcel down into the empty canoe. The jig was up.

"Jordie Jones!" chorused the two teachers.

The coach was holding onto his head with both hands. "How did you get here? *Why* are you here? *Please* go away!"

Bruno ran up. "Sir, remember what he did for our team! He risked his whole career so we could beat York Academy! You can't send him back!"

"You bet I can't!" howled Flynn. "Not unless a cab happens to come by! We're at the corner of Nothing and Nowhere!"

"We can't keep him, either," put in Mr. Fudge. "He's a star. Half the world's going to be looking for him."

"That's no problem," said Jordie brightly. "I called my parents while you were eating."

"And they said it's okay?" asked the coach eagerly.

"Well, not exactly. They weren't home. So I said don't worry on the answering machine."

"Oh, they'll love that!" groaned Flynn sarcastically. "That'll put their minds completely at ease!"

"Sir," piped up Calvin. "I volunteer."

"For what?"

"I'm more at home in these woods than in my own living room. I'll get Jordie to town and be back here in an hour."

"Fihzgart, it's fifty kilometres!"

Calvin shrugged. "An hour and a half."

Mr. Fudge spoke up. "He *does* have a point. Maybe Jones and I could hike back to the highway and, once I see him safely on his way home, I'll rejoin you."

Flynn mopped his brow. "Let me think. I'm the more experienced navigator, so I should go with Jordie. But I'm the experienced camper, too, so I should stay with the group. I guess it has to be you."

Mr. Fudge nodded.

Flynn pulled out the notebook and squatted down by the canoe. "Look, following these directions in reverse will take you back to where the bus let us off. Then you're only a few kilometres from the main road, and maybe you can grab a lift to town. I'll just make a quick copy for myself, and you can start right away. You'll want to make it in before dark, stay over and rejoin us tomorrow." He tore out the page with the directions and, using the grocery sack as a table, began to copy the information.

Jordie was devastated. "It's only a few days! No one'll know the difference!"

"Aw, come on, sir," said Bruno. "Can't you let him stay?"

"This isn't a game, Walton. There could be a major manhunt going on! Not to mention that the wilderness survival trip is an important part of your education!" He leaned on the grocery sack and turned to regard Bruno sternly. "He goes home, and that's that."

There was a gravelly, grinding sound, and the canoe lurched under his weight. Surprised, the coach jumped back, dropping papers, pen and compass to the small boat's floor. The craft slid away from him, its smooth bottom slipping easily across the marshy ground toward the slope that led to the lake.

"The boat!" cried Mr. Fudge in horror.

"The directions!" bellowed Flynn.

"The *food*!" shrieked Wilbur.

In an act of desperation, the coach launched himself like a football tackler at the sliding canoe. He overshot his target, landing heavily in it, flat on his face. That was all the momentum the small craft needed. It jolted over the edge of the slope and rocketed down the hill like a roller coaster, bouncing off boulders and bushes. Mr. Flynn cried out in terror as the S.S. *Drown-in-the-Woods* picked up speed, hurtling for the lake. Mr. Fudge and all the campers tore down the hill after it.

"Coach! Jump!"

"Look out for that branch!"

"Save the food!"

Just before the water, a large curved rock jutted out of the embankment. It loomed like a ramp in the path of the speeding canoe. Coach and craft hit the smooth surface of the rock like an Olympic champion on a ski jump. Flynn lost his grip and flew straight upward, arms and legs windmilling. The canoe shot off the end of the rock, sailed gracefully through the air and bottomed neatly into the water, seven metres from shore. Its forward momentum carried it smoothly and steadily out toward the centre of the lake.

Bruno was first to reach Coach Flynn, who lay in a heap in the soft mud at the water's edge. "Sir! Sir, speak to me!"

Dazed, Flynn sat up, cradling his right ankle. "Ow! I think I hurt my foot! Where's the canoe?"

"Out there!" puffed Mr. Fudge.

The coach followed his pointing finger and sighed with relief. "Thank heaven! If that rock had ripped a hole in the bottom, say good-bye to our food and our directions!"

"I hope it doesn't drift too far," commented Mr. Fudge. "That's a mighty cold swim."

The coach hugged his injured foot. "What choice do we have? Without that stuff, we're dead!"

Eleven pairs of eyes watched in agony as the canoe, still sailing gently across the placid lake, rode lower and lower in the water, until only the tiny point of its stern and the top of the grocery sack were still visible. Then the S.S. *Drown-in-the-Woods* slipped silently below the surface and was gone without a ripple.

No one said anything for a long time. They all stared at the calm waters that had claimed their canoe, their supplies and their way home.

Pete Anderson was first to break the silence. "Hey," he said, his voice a mixture of disbelief and dread. "We really *are* going to die in the woods!"

Chapter 12

The Rescue Mission

Seth Dinkman peered through the lens of camera two, lining up a long shot of the three Macdonald Hall dormitories. Suddenly the image was replaced by a blur of white sports clothes.

"Seth, I have to talk to you," came Goose Golden's voice, agitated as usual.

Dinkman turned to his cameraman. "Move the camera. That was the ugliest shot I've ever seen."

"Come on, Seth! This is important!" Golden grabbed the director by the collar and dropped his voice to a whisper. "I can't find J.J.!"

"You couldn't find Russia if you started out in downtown Moscow. Leave me alone."

"He isn't in his trailer," Golden went on, "and the commissary people say he wasn't at breakfast *or* lunch."

Dinkman raised his megaphone. *"Okay, sports fans, take five. I have to fulfil my life's true purpose and waste my time on this idiot."* He walked the manager over to a secluded spot. "Was his bed slept in?"

Golden nodded. "Yeah, but — "

"No buts," Dinkman interrupted. "We've been keeping the kid tied up twenty-four hours a day, and when we ran out of interviews he escaped to be with his friends, that's all. He's around somewhere."

"Then why can't I find him?"

Dinkman fixed him with a stern look. "Have you ruled out stupidity? Look, now it's daytime, the sun's out and I'm busy. When it's dark, you can bother me. I'm not guaranteeing I won't rip your lungs out, but you can try. Now, go away. Jordie's fine."

* * *

The diagnosis came from Elmer Drimsdale. He examined the coach's bruised and swollen foot and pronounced, "Sir, you have three fractured metatarsals."

"Elmer, speak English!" piped Bruno.

"Mr. Flynn has a broken foot."

The coach groaned and lay back on his sleeping bag. He even looked out through the trees down to the lake to see if maybe, just maybe, the lost canoe had resurfaced and was floating toward shore. No luck.

"So what do we do?" asked Mr. Fudge.

Elmer blinked. "Do?"

"About my foot!" raged the coach.

"I have no idea," replied the genius. "The practical side of science is not one of my strengths."

"Don't worry, Coach!" cried Calvin. "I know *exactly* what to do! First, I kill a water buffalo — "

Flynn was becoming hysterical. *"Does anybody know how to set a broken bone?"*

Timidly Jordie stepped forward. "I think I might."

"What do you mean, 'might,'" growled Mr. Flynn. "We're talking about my *foot*!"

"Well, when I was in *Young Paramedics*, the producers hired a first-aid expert to teach us how to treat wounds and set bones so it would seem natural on camera." He looked worried. "I never had a real patient, though."

Flynn looked around desperately. "Anybody else?"

There were no volunteers. Mr. Fudge looked embarrassed, blank and helpless.

Jordie supervised the cutting of two splints from a nearby tree — a large flat one for below the foot, and a smaller, slightly curved piece for above. Padding the wood with gauze bandages, he put the upper and lower pieces in place and tied them together firmly with more gauze to keep the foot immobilized. Then he wrapped a foam pad from one of the sleeping bags around Flynn's lower leg, placed a flat stone under the whole arrangement to keep the injury slightly raised and sat back to admire his handiwork.

"How does that feel, Coach?"

"Not bad," said Flynn in slight surprise. "It hurts like crazy, but it feels nice and firm. The point is, how can we send somebody for help when we lost our directions back to the highway?"

Calvin laughed out loud. "No sweat! What a bunch of tenderfeet you guys are! An experienced woodsman always marks his trail!"

Hope flared in the eyes of the two teachers.

"You left a trail? Way to go, Fihzgart!" cheered the coach.

"Of course I did!" Calvin confirmed heartily. "It starts right here. There's the first marker. All the way from the road, I dropped a peanut every five paces."

Ten voices chorused, "A *peanut*?!"

"Yeah. What's wrong with peanuts?"

As if on cue, a red squirrel scampered out of the bush, snatched up the trail-marking peanut and disappeared up a tree.

"Well," said Larry dryly, "maybe we can follow a trail of fat squirrels."

"Big joke," muttered Wilbur miserably. "I could have had that peanut."

"Don't worry," said Mr. Fudge confidently. "I've got a compass. If I head south, I'm bound to hit the highway. Is Jones coming with me?"

The coach sighed. "Without directions we can't risk it. He'll just have to wait here until help comes."

"Take me with you, Mr. Fudge!" begged Calvin. "I'll guide you through!"

Flynn's face twisted. "Fihzgart stays here. We might need another dead water buffalo."

* * *

By nightfall, there was still no sign of rescue. Mr. Fudge had been gone for over seven hours.

"Gee, I sure hope nothing's happened to him," said Boots anxiously.

Coach Flynn was forcing himself to be cheerful. "Don't worry about Mr. Fudge. He's a big boy and can take care of himself. It's a long way, that's all."

The three big tents were already set up, and a roaring campfire cast a warm glow over the clearing. Coach Flynn had supervised the entire operation from flat on his back on his sleeping bag. Not being able to help frustrated him. Of the boys, the only one who knew the first thing about camping was Jordie Jones. The star had never camped in his life but had appeared in at least three wilderness movies, picking up the odd skill here and there.

The only food not at the bottom of the lake was a sack of self-rising flour and a jar of shortening. Following Mr. Flynn's recipe, Jordie and Boots made a passable batch of bannock. The coach gave a solemn lecture about how this was the last of the supplies, and they should ration themselves. But in three minutes, every last crumb was gone. Dessert was a shared package of LifeSavers from the linty pocket of Pete Anderson. When that was eaten, the wilderness survival trip was officially out of food.

The very thought of it devastated Wilbur Hackenschleimer. To him, foodlessness was the lowest state to which humanity could sink. He sat forlornly on a rock, gazing bleakly into the fire. "I can't believe how fast this happened. Just yesterday we had meat loaf, mashed potatoes, gravy — it seems like a million years ago. I had indigestion. Today indigestion is something I can only *dream* about!"

"Don't worry," Calvin assured him. "Tomorrow we'll all be having steak!"

Wilbur glared at him with venom. "What are you going to kill this time — a butcher shop?"

Calvin was unperturbed. "First thing in the morning, I'll fashion a crude crossbow — "

Wilbur lost control. "Shut up, you idiot, or tomorrow we'll be having moron stew!"

Bruno broke up the fight. "Come on. Lay off Calvin. He honestly thinks he's going to save our lives."

"Hey," called Flynn, "our lives don't need saving. Everything's under control."

There was a halfhearted chorus of agreement.

"So where's Mr. Fudge with the rescuers?" queried Mark, aiming his video camera at the worried faces sitting in the deep red glow of the fire.

"They've probably decided not to come in the dark," the coach explained. "They'll be here first thing tomorrow — and they'll bring breakfast," he added, looking at Wilbur.

There were no songs around the campfire for the wilderness survival trip that night. No ghost stories were exchanged, no practical jokes played. Once the boys were in their tents, trying to drift into an uneasy sleep, the night noises of the forest struck instant terror into the hearts of everyone.

"Hoot! Hoot!"

Boots sat bolt upright in his sleeping bag. "What was that?"

"Why, the mating call of the great horned owl, of course," explained Elmer. He formed his mouth into a circle and produced exactly the same sound. An answering hoot came from the darkness. Elmer switched on his flashlight and began to make notes.

Bruno rolled over. "Since you speak owl, Elm, how about telling that guy to shut up so we can get some sleep?"

But the zoologist in Elmer was aroused. He gave seven bird-calls in rapid succession, then paused, scribbling as the responses came in from Algonquin Park.

Jordie propped himself up on his elbows. "Why can't you do this tomorrow?"

"These are night birds," said Elmer seriously. "Naturally, in the daylight, I'll be doing an extensive study of diurnal creatures."

Bruno yawned. "Hey, why don't you tell us all about it, Elm? That should put us to sleep."

"Pipe down in there," came Mr. Flynn's voice from the next tent.

"Coach," spoke up Pete, "Wilbur's drooling in his sleep again."

"Hey!" hissed Boots suddenly. "There's something out there!"

"Ah, you hear it too," said Elmer. "The faint, high-pitched whistle of the hoary bat. Excellent."

"Not that sound! The other one! Something's in the bushes!"

"Oh, that," said Elmer, disappointed. "That's just an eighty-kilo adult human walking quickly through heavy underbrush."

"The rescue team!" chorused Bruno, Boots and Jordie.

In seconds, the nine campers were out of their tents, squinting around the clearing in the light of the dying fire. The rustling of leaves and snapping of branches grew louder until, finally, the bushes parted, and a bedraggled, disoriented figure burst into camp. It was Mr. Fudge.

He stared at them in dismay. "What are you doing here? This is the highway!"

* * *

Sun-up brought a new development to the camp of the wilderness survival trip. When Bruno Walton dug into his luggage in search of warm clothes and dry boots, he found Bermuda shorts, his Sunday suit, two neckties, beach sandals, his

Toronto Blue Jays sun visor and a sleeveless basketball jersey.

"Oh, no," moaned Boots. "I knew I should have checked your things after I saw the way you packed!"

"This is no problem," said Bruno airily. "I'll just borrow some extra stuff."

So it was that when Bruno headed down to the lake for the morning's fishing, he was decked out in Elmer's sweatshirt, Boots's jeans and Calvin's long underwear, which were squeezing the life out of him so that he walked in a constricted gunfighter stance. The boots were donated by Coach Flynn, who had no further need of footwear. These were several sizes too large, even with three pairs of socks (Mark's, Dave's and Wilbur's), so Bruno stuffed a tie in each toe.

"I knew they'd come in handy," he grinned.

They had no boat, so they fished from the ramp rock that had launched the S.S. *Drown-in-the-Woods* on its trip to the bottom of the lake.

Calvin was the first to get a bite, and he was jubilant. "The true woodsman comes through again, to bring food to his starving companions!" Furiously he reeled in his catch, a small brook trout about ten centimetres long.

"Salvelinus fontinalis," pronounced Elmer.

"It's humongous!" Calvin raved. "What a whopper! The biggest fish ever caught in these waters!" He grabbed the end of the line, took one look at the razor-sharp hook piercing the trout's mouth and fainted, his breath leaving him in a slow gasp.

Bruno and Boots toted Calvin and his prize up the slope to camp and laid him out beside Flynn.

Calvin came to just in time to see Coach Flynn slit his fish up the middle to clean it. It was too much for the brave woodsman. He passed out again.

The fishing was excellent. Every few minutes, a burst of cheering would come from the lake. Within the hour, the wilderness survival trip was sitting down to a hearty breakfast of fresh fish.

Rested and fed, Mr. Fudge was ready to make another stab at finding the highway.

"Be careful not to get turned around again," Flynn cautioned. "If you feel you're going out of a straight line, check your compass and adjust your course due south."

The Housemaster, his face scratched by branches, his expression nowhere near as confident as yesterday, gave them the thumbs-up signal and off he went.

Wilbur asked the most important question on his mind right after breakfast. "What's for lunch?"

"Fish," said Coach Flynn cheerfully. "It's the only nutrition around."

"On the contrary," said Elmer. "There is a smorgasbord of food all about us."

"Well, yeah," Flynn admitted dubiously. "But I don't think anybody's really interested in — "

"*I* am!" Wilbur interrupted, looking anxiously around the clearing. "A guy's got to have variety. Okay, Elmer, where's the smorgasbord?"

"Let's see," Elmer began. "Mushrooms, acorns, algae, bark, roots, certain edible grubs — "

Wilbur grabbed a fishing rod. "Let's get to it."

* * *

When the movie crew broke for lunch that day, Seth Dinkman and Goose Golden met in a quiet corner of the commissary trailer.

There were enormous dark circles under the manager's eyes from lack of sleep, and his white linen tennis outfit was one big wrinkle from tossing and turning, fully dressed, on the couch in Jordie's trailer.

"I knew it! He's been kidnapped!"

"Shhh!" admonished the director. "He hasn't been kidnapped. I just got off the phone with his mother. She says he left her a message that he's taking off for a few days, and he'll be back."

Golden was not consoled. "That's crazy! He's never pulled anything like this before! He's only a little kid!"

"He's a little kid who can get V.I.P. treatment anywhere in the world on the strength of his face," added Dinkman. "You think anybody would ask any questions if he checked into a hotel? Listen, Goose, we smothered him and pushed him around, and he's fighting back. Meanwhile, I've got our security people making discreet inquiries in Toronto."

"Have you called the police?" quavered Golden.

"Are you crazy? If the police know, the press'll get wind of it, and that's all we need! This kind of bad publicity can bury a movie! So you keep your big mouth shut and stay out of sight. Just the look on your face would tell a reporter something's up."

"Well, we could at least ask Sturgeon," the manager persisted. "He always knows what's going on — "

"Don't even *think* about it!" rasped the director. "Sturgeon would just call the cops. We've got to keep this quiet!"

"But I'm so worried!" whined Goose.

"Don't be. If I know Jordie, he's probably living it up at the best hotel in town."

Chapter 13

The Media Circus

By noon the next day, two things were becoming apparent at the campsite in Algonquin Park. One, eating fish three meals a day wore thin very quickly. And two, Mr. Fudge was probably lost again, and help was not on the way.

It had rained all the previous night, and two of the three tents had sprung leaks. Tension in the camp was steadily mounting. Tempers flared, and when the boys weren't snapping at each other, there were long silences. Most preferred the arguing.

Mr. Flynn tried walking, with two tree branches as crutches, but it was no use. His injury and the muddiness of the ground were too much to overcome. "Boys," he said solemnly, "I don't want to alarm you, but I think you've all figured out that we're in a bit of a situation here. Just remember that we're in no danger if we stay put. We've got shelter, water and a steady food supply. At the absolute worst, when we're not at the road to meet the bus day after tomorrow, the alarm will go out, and we'll be rescued then. Comments?"

"We could get to the road, sir!" promised Calvin. "I could carry you!"

"Thanks, Fihzgart. Anybody else?" His eyes fell on Bruno's morose face. "Well, Walton? Obviously you've got something to say."

Bruno hung his head. "I was just thinking about all the rotten jokes I played on Mr. Fudge over the last couple of years. I put a lizard in his bed, I ordered him a pizza, I booby-trapped his toilet — "

"That was you?" blurted Pete. "Good one!"

Bruno looked guilty. "Well, it just seems kind of weird that I never got a chance to say I was sorry."

"He's not dead!" exploded Flynn.

"It was raining pretty hard last night — " ventured Jordie.

"Your imaginations are getting the better of you," the coach lectured. "Look at Drimsdale here. He isn't letting a few problems get him down."

"On the contrary, sir," said Elmer. "This has all been most fascinating. I saw a rare Acadian flycatcher today."

"Now, after lunch," said Flynn, "we're going to start building a raft."

"Great idea!" approved Calvin. "I'll paddle out of here, and when I reach Greenland, I'll airlift help!"

"It's not transportation," Flynn replied patiently. "I figure we put an SOS signal on it and float it out into the middle of the lake for any passing aircraft to see."

Wilbur was put in charge of the tree-chopping detail. His instructions: "Pick small maple saplings, stand well clear and don't let Fihzgart anywhere near the axe."

Bruno, Boots and Jordie were sent straight from a lunch of fish to catch fish for dinner.

Bruno dropped his line in the water. "Well, Cutesy? Still glad you came on Die-in-the-Woods?"

Jordie grinned. "It's not so bad. I feel kind of lousy that most of this is my fault, though. I hope you guys don't flunk the trip."

Bruno looked haunted. "Hey, you don't think they'll make us do it over till we get it right?!"

"I doubt it," said Boots. "I'll bet we're doing more real surviving than anybody else ever did."

"If we survive," Bruno added. "Think we'll be rescued?"

"No problem," said Jordie. "If the school, the police, the forest rangers, the Coast Guard and the army don't find us, Goose will be here."

"Coach Flynn doesn't think there's any danger," commented Boots. He scratched his head. "That's what bothers me. If we're all safe and sound — why do we need an SOS raft?"

* * *

Goose Golden lay on the couch in Jordie's darkened trailer, a cold cloth on his head, a hot water bottle clutched to his middle. The strain of the last three days had sapped every gram of his strength. No one could blame him for slipping up in front of that reporter yesterday. His mind was operating at triple speed! And at that pace, who could screen every little thing that came out of his mouth? Besides, the reporter hadn't noticed it. The secret was still safe.

There was an enormous crash as the trailer door was wrenched open and slammed shut, and there fumed Seth Dinkman, an avenging angel. He switched on the light and shoved a newspaper under Goose's nose. The banner headline read:

Dinkman was raging. "Only two people knew about this, and I didn't tell! Who does that leave? Queen Elizabeth? No. Zorro? No. Shamu the Killer Whale?"

"It was me," Golden confessed. "It just slipped out. I'm not myself lately."

"Well, if you're not yourself, why couldn't you be someone intelligent? Do you know how many reporters we've got out there? A million, that's how many!"

"What are we going to do?" quavered the manager.

"This afternoon I'm calling a press conference," announced Dinkman, "just as soon as the rest of those bloodsuckers arrive! Jordie is *not* missing! He's on vacation for a few days!"

"But he *is* missing!" wailed Golden.

"This is the official story," Dinkman insisted. "We know exactly where he is, but we're not telling the press so the poor kid can have some privacy. Anybody who prints anything different gets sued for libel."

"Do you think they'll believe it?" asked Golden.

"They'll have to. The studio's backing us up, Jordie's parents are backing us up — we're solid." He pressed his index finger against the manager's pancreas. "And if you blow this, I'm going to pull your tongue out and run a steamroller over it so you'll have to fold for two hours just to get it back in your big mouth!"

* * *

Up a tall tree in Miss Scrimmage's apple orchard, Cathy Burton lowered her binoculars and frowned. It had been three days since Jordie Jones had set foot outside his trailer. At first she'd thought the star was confined to his bed under doctor's orders, perhaps due to complications with the healing of his eye. But Jordie never came out for meals, and no food ever went in. It didn't make sense. Nobody fasted to cure a black eye. Maybe he was so sick that he couldn't eat at all.

"Pssst! Cathy! Get down here!" Diane stood at the base of the tree, beckoning urgently.

"I'm watching for Jordie," Cathy called down.

"Well, you're not going to see him!" Diane announced tragically. "He's gone!"

"Gone?!" Cathy dropped like a cat from the tree. "What do you mean 'gone'?"

"Wilma just heard it on the radio! He's disappeared!"

Cathy stared at her. Slowly a grin of sheer delight took over her face.

Diane was horrified. "How can you stand there smiling? Don't you understand? He's *vanished*! No one knows where he is!"

"I do," grinned Cathy.

Diane was still raving. "He could be in trouble! Or hurt! or *dead*!" She stopped short. "*You* do?"

"It's so obvious! I can't believe I didn't see it before! We last saw him three days ago, and the very next morning — "

"Die-in-the-Woods!" shrieked Diane.

"Right," said Cathy, pleased. "He's gone camping with Bruno and Boots. And it looks like they didn't tell anybody, or no one would be saying he's disappeared. Now, what does that mean?"

"He's safe!" sighed Diane.

"And we're the only ones who know where to find him," Cathy added.

"That's right!" said Diane excitedly. "We have to call the radio station — "

"Are you crazy? We call *nobody*! Jordie's up there, with no cameras, no directors, no managers, no security — just a bunch of guys and a couple of teachers! When we get to him, he's ours!"

Diane gawked at her roommate. "How are *we* going to get to him? For one thing, Miss Scrimmage is taking us to Montreal tomorrow with the Baking Club!"

"There's going to be a slight change of itinerary," Cathy replied smugly.

"Get real! Miss Scrimmage may be a little out to lunch, but she knows the difference between Montreal and Algonquin Park!"

Cathy's eyes gleamed. "Yeah, but she doesn't know the difference between the *road* to Montreal and the *road* to Algonquin Park. Think, Diane! Miss Scrimmage is hopeless with maps, so she types out her directions, one turn at a time. All we have to do is swap our turns for hers."

Diane's head was spinning. "But we don't *have* any turns! That park is a humongous place, and we have no idea what part of it they went to!"

Cathy shrugged. "The bus company knows. I'll call up and weasel it out of them. Come on, Diane! You should be bouncing off the ceiling! We're finally going to meet Jordie Jones!"

"Well, I guess so, but — "

"No buts, kiddo! Pack your long johns! We're going camping!"

* * *

Mr. Sturgeon drove his blue Ford north on Highway 48 toward Macdonald Hall. It was late afternoon, and he was returning from an exhausting day of meetings with the Board of Directors in Toronto. A good dinner was on his mind, followed by a quiet evening with his paper, a hot bath and then into bed for a solid eight hours sleep. Why, he could feel himself starting to unwind already.

He turned right onto the Macdonald Hall grounds, and his relaxation shattered into a million pieces. The wide circular driveway in front of the Faculty Building was a parking lot, jammed with cars, trucks and vans. The Headmaster could make out at least six TV mobile units. There was no question about it. The media was back at Macdonald Hall and in greater force than ever.

Grimacing with irritation, he threaded his way along the drive to his cottage on the south lawn. His wife was waiting for him, pacing up and down on the porch. Spying the Ford, she rushed forward to meet her husband, waving the afternoon paper in front of the windshield. The headline blazoned:

WHERE IS JORDIE JONES?

He knew instantly. If Jones was missing, it meant that he had joined Walton and O'Neal on the wilderness survival trip. And Flynn and Fudge, cut off from the world and not willing to leave the rest of the boys with inadequate supervision, had wisely decided to wait out the five days, treating the star simply as an extra camper. It all fit. What a useless, needless, unbearable complication!

With a screech of gears, he threw the Ford into reverse and

backed all the way across the campus to the east lawn. There he found Goose Golden, sitting despondently outside Jordie's trailer.

The Headmaster got out of his car and approached on foot. "Good afternoon, Golden."

"J.J.'s missing!" blurted the manager. He clapped both hands over his mouth. "I mean — uh — no comment."

Mr. Sturgeon smiled thinly. "Perhaps I can put your mind at rest. I know where young Jones is, and I assure you he's safe and sound."

The manager rocketed off the stoop and froze just short of enveloping the Headmaster in a bear hug. "Where? Where is he?"

Mr. Sturgeon looked around. "Perhaps we might summon Dinkman. I would much rather not have to tell this twice."

Golden shook his head. "Seth's holding a press conference. He's trying to convince the reporters J.J.'s just on vacation."

Mr. Sturgeon sighed heavily. "It is, in essence, the truth. Eight of my students are away on a wilderness survival trip. Jones is with them."

The manager recoiled in horror. "Survival? As in *not dying*? But he's only a little kid!"

"My eight are hardly professional lumberjacks," said the Headmaster in stern reproof. "They are well supervised and perfectly safe. You'll have your client back on Saturday."

"But that's two more days! Anything could happen in two days in the wilderness! He could be attacked by wolves! He could fall in a hole! He could get bitten by a tsetse fly! He could catch Dutch elm disease!"

"Don't be absurd, Golden. Only trees get Dutch elm disease."

"Well, what if a sick tree falls on him, then? He'd be crushed like a bug! I want him back!"

"And you shall have him," said Mr. Sturgeon icily. "On Saturday. Now, please pass this information on to Dinkman. Good day." He returned to his car and drove off toward the south lawn.

Golden sat back down on the stoop, even more agitated than before. The thought of J.J. out there in the wilds was almost worse than not knowing the boy's whereabouts at all. This was torture.

Look at him! He was hugging himself to keep his hands from shaking, rocking back and forth — he was a wreck! He began mumbling his mantra over and over again, but the relaxation of meditation would not come. He entered the trailer to try some of the primal scream therapy recommended by his psychiatrist, but today all it gave him was a sore throat. He did the twenty-minute workout, switching to the thirty-minute and finally the forty-minute. Nothing could calm him. He tried the TV, but found only a *Cutesy Newbar* rerun, which was too painful to watch. Poor J.J.

At last, exhausted, he stretched out on the couch. Soon the exertion, combined with his anxious days and sleepless nights, took its toll. Goose Golden was out like a light.

About half an hour later, Seth Dinkman arrived to give his report on the press conference. "Well, they didn't really buy it, but at least now we've got them thinking — " He caught sight of Golden snoring softly on the couch.

It figured. Dinkman had just been put through the shredder by every reporter on earth, and here was Goose, taking a nap. Diabolically, he toyed with the idea of waking the manager by means of a bucket of ice water. No, that was a bad idea. Better to leave well enough alone. When Goose was sleeping, at least he wasn't shooting off his mouth to the press.

* * *

"Tea's ready, William."

Mr. Sturgeon was standing in his living room, glaring out the picture window at his darkening campus. It was a carnival, that's what it was! He'd already counted six pizza delivery trucks, two for Chinese food and a visit from the local chicken joint. There was that tall, red-haired reporter from some New York newspaper bedding down in the backseat of his Volkswagen, his great flat feet sticking out the window! A mobile unit from one of the Toronto stations had actually stretched a clothesline from the top of their van to the out-stretched hand on the statue of Sir John A. Macdonald in front of the Faculty Building. On it flapped socks and underwear. They were doing their laundry! All over, picnics were going on, some of them raucous. One radio crew had had the gall to fill the barrel of the War of 1812 cannon that stood on the front lawn with ice cubes to keep their drinks cold!

Disgusted, he turned away from the window, walked into the kitchen and dropped heavily into a chair. "Mildred, they're not leaving. Not even to sleep."

She poured two cups of tea. "We don't have to put up with this, you know, William. This is private property. We *can* call the police."

"I'm sorely tempted," he sighed, "but I don't dare. They smell news, and if we kick them off the campus, it'll only provide them with incentive to sneak back on. They'll move their zoo out to the highway, which is *not* private property. And then we'll be under siege, with police patrolling the perimeters, asking my teachers to show identification just to get to class. That's not the atmosphere I want for our boys. I'd rather have the media circus than an armed camp."

At that moment, the background music on the kitchen radio faded, and an announcer's voice came on:

"And now for the eight o'clock news. Actor Jordie Jones is still nowhere to be found since he disappeared two days ago from location filming at the Macdonald Hall private school for boys, northeast of Toronto. Although studio sources cling to the story that Jones is simply on vacation, sightings of the young star continue to pour in from all over southern Ontario. The latest comes from Sarnia farmer Angus McPeach, who claims he saw Jones board a UFO in his bean field about noon today . . ."

Mrs. Sturgeon threw up her arms in frustration. "These media people are incorrigible! They crawl all over the campus on the pretext of finding the truth, and then they report such utter claptrap! Is there *anything* that would stop them?"

"Nothing short of Jordie Jones himself, dead or alive," replied her husband morosely. Suddenly he snapped to attention, surprised by his own words. "Of course! If I can produce the boy, there will be no more mystery and no more investigations!"

"But that can't happen until the wilderness survival trip comes back on Saturday."

"Yes it can," he replied, jaw set with determination. "Jones returns tomorrow. With me."

His wife was shocked. "William, don't even think of it! That's a long drive and a gruelling hike through dense woods — both ways!"

"Do you think I'm looking forward to it?" the Headmaster demanded. "I haven't gone on the wilderness survival trip in twenty-five years. I hated it then, and in all that time, I have undergone no change of heart. The only thing worse than going to Algonquin Park tomorrow is staying here and watching those sensation seekers use our cannon as an ice bucket!"

"But William — "

He was adamant. "Prepare my union suit, Mildred. I'm going on Die-in-the-Woods."

Chapter 14

A Cry in the Woods

Miss Scrimmage's driving would have earned her the pole position at the Indianapolis 500, so by nine o'clock the next morning, the Baking Club was burning northeast on Highway 11, heading for Route 60, which led to Algonquin Park.

The Headmistress glanced in the rearview mirror at the five girls riding with her in the school's minivan. "Everybody cheery and comfortable?"

"Oh, yes, Miss Scrimmage!" raved Cathy. "I'm so glad I joined the Baking Club!"

Miss Scrimmage smiled happily. "Mind you, you look awfully crowded back there. I still don't understand why everyone brought so much luggage. It's only a short trip."

The girls exchanged conspiratorial smiles. Their large suit-cases concealed sleeping bags and other camping gear. Maybe Miss Scrimmage was going to Montreal, but they were heading for Jordie Jones.

Miss Scrimmage whizzed past a tractor-trailer at nearly double the speed limit. "How odd," she frowned, gearing down. "None of these signs mentions Montreal. I hope we haven't taken a wrong turn." She consulted her directions (revised and retyped by Cathy the night before). "Well, this is the road, all right. Very strange."

"Tell us again about proper manners in an authentic French pastry shop," suggested Diane.

"An excellent idea!" the Headmistress agreed, accelerating. "Of course, we'll be ordering in French, and the pronunciation of the letter "R" is crucial. Montreal waiters can be merciless on pronunciation. Why, I remember once . . . "

* * *

When Mr. Sturgeon stepped out of his cottage that morning, none of his students would have recognized him. He had traded in his usual conservative grey business suit for baggy khakis, held up by elastic suspenders which stretched tightly over his thick red-and-black-plaid flannel shirt. The boots on his feet laced halfway to the knees, and on his head perched a fur-lined leather hunting cap with earflaps. Only his steel-rimmed glasses gave away the fact that this was the stern, dignified Headmaster of Macdonald Hall.

He got into his car and started the engine, then ripped the hunting cap from his head and tossed it on the seat beside him. A glance toward home showed his wife in the picture window, shaking her finger at him. With a sigh, he replaced the cap.

He started off slowly down the crowded driveway. Delivery trucks with coffee and doughnuts were already beginning to arrive for the awakening reporters. He hadn't set one tire on the highway yet and already he was in a traffic jam.

He was about to pull out onto the road when a voice cried, "Wait! Wait! You can't go yet!" A streak of white overtook the car from the left side and leaptout in front. Goose Golden, toupee askew, pressed both hands against the hood of the Ford, as though he expected to keep Mr. Sturgeon off the highway by brute force.

The Headmaster rolled down his window. "What is it, Golden? I'm in a hurry."

"Take me with you!" the manager begged.

"Whatever for? I'm only going down the road for a litre of milk." Even as the words came out of his mouth, he felt an utter fool. No one shopped for milk dressed like a reject from *Field & Stream.*

"You're going for J.J.!" said Golden urgently. "I have to come with you!" Even as Mr. Sturgeon was opening his mouth to refuse, the agent lunged for the passenger door, wrenched it open and parked himself on the seat, buckling his safety belt. He gave the Headmaster an ingratiating smile. "Nice hat. I've always wanted one of those."

"Kindly leave my car, Golden."

The manager crossed his arms. "J.J. needs me!"

Mr. Sturgeon grimaced. "You're not exactly dressed for a wilderness trek. Please go about your business and allow me to go about mine."

"J.J. *is* my business — my *only* business."

The Headmaster shook his head in resignation. "Very well. I suppose you have as much right as anyone." He put the car back into gear and turned onto the highway.

* * *

Following her directions, Miss Scrimmage took the exit onto Route 60 but almost immediately squealed the van into a dangerous U-turn.

"Idiot!" howled a man in a black Camaro. He had slammed on his brakes at the last second to avoid a collision.

"Why are we turning around, Miss Scrimmage?" asked Cathy. Diane and the other girls looked nervous.

"This is definitely the wrong way!" she said, flustered. "The road to Montreal is a big highway! This is just two lanes. It looks awfully rural — "

"Maybe we're taking the northern route to see more of the countryside," suggested Diane hopefully.

Miss Scrimmage stopped dead. Behind them, the Camaro screeched to a halt again, eight centimetres off the van's back bumper. The driver stuck his head out the window. "What are you — *crazy*, lady?"

Miss Scrimmage scratched her head. "Well, perhaps that was my thinking," she mused over the din of the Camaro's horn behind them. Finally she reached a decision and wheeled the van hard about, just as the Camaro attempted to drive around her. Both vehicles stopped, facing each other head-on, front bumpers a centimetre apart.

Now it was Miss Scrimmage's turn to honk. "Sir, you are blocking my path," she called out the window. "What is more, you are on the wrong side of the road."

Face flaming, the other motorist emitted a stream of insults and abuse.

Miss Scrimmage never got beyond "You lunatic . . ."

"Well, I never!" she exclaimed, wheeling around the Camaro

and tearing off down the highway at breakneck speed. She began a lecture to her girls on the ladylike way to deal with "a horribly abusive ignoramus who was probably born in a barn and drives unsafely besides." She was eighty kilometres down the road before she realized that she didn't know where she was going.

The van screeched to a halt in a cloud of burning rubber.

"What's the problem, Miss Scrimmage?" asked Diane.

The Headmistress looked haunted. She peered through the windshield as though hoping to spy Montreal waiting right around the next bend. Instead, she got northeastern Ontario, lots of it, as far as the eye could see. "We can't go this way," she said softly.

Cathy spoke up. "Well, can we go *this* way?" She pointed back in the direction they had come from. Miss Scrimmage looked in the rearview mirror. The scene was almost exactly the same. "No," she barely whispered.

Cathy leaned forward and patted the Headmistress sympathetically on the shoulder. "Don't worry, Miss Scrimmage. We know where we're going."

Miss Scrimmage put the van in gear.

* * *

"Well, sure, it's sort of an okay raft, I guess," said Calvin, "but how come you didn't use *my* tree?"

"Yours was too small," said Coach Flynn.

"Too small?!" roared Calvin. "It was the mightiest tree in the forest!"

That got a big laugh.

"You cut it down with the scissors on your Swiss Army knife," Wilbur pointed out.

"It was a colossus!"

"It was a twig."

The SOS raft was now finished, and all the boys were pretty proud of themselves. It was made up of saplings about ten centimetres in diameter, tied together with twine from the survival kits and measured a little more than three metres square. On one end Bruno had scratched the inscription S.S. *Drown-in-the-Woods II.*

Bruno, Boots and Jordie were hard at work cutting the letters *H, E, L* and *P* out of Wilbur's bright-red long underwear. They would secure these to the top of the raft with pine gum, as Jordie had done in last summer's blockbuster movie *Marooned in the Swamp.*

"You should have done *SOS*," grumbled Wilbur. "You might run out of material with four letters, and you're not getting my T-shirt."

Bruno emitted a bark of laughter. "Are you kidding? We could put *Assistance Required as Soon as Possible* and still have enough stuff left over to cut out all our names!"

"Very funny."

Once finished, the raft would go out into the middle of the lake to shout its message to the sky and, with luck, to rescuers. If that didn't work, Calvin was still volunteering to paddle to Greenland, and no hard feelings.

"What if it doesn't float?" asked Pete nervously.

"Then it'll sink," said Larry. "At least it'll have a lot of company down there."

"Of course it'll float, Anderson," snapped Flynn. "Wood floats."

"Hey, Elmer," piped Boots, "how about that one?" He was referring to a loud hissing sound that seemed to come from the woods all around them.

"Cicadas," said Elmer. "Probably the first ones of the season. They don't usually appear this far north until June."

Ever since the night of the birdcalls, it had become a game around camp to see if Elmer could identify every single noise the forest had to offer. So far, the genius hadn't been stumped once.

"Are you sure he really knows all that stuff?" Jordie whispered to Boots. "If he made it up, we wouldn't know the difference."

"You just don't know Elmer," Boots replied. "He's smart enough to know that junk and a hundred times more, but he doesn't have the imagination to fake one answer."

The chirping call of a bird rang through the clearing. All eyes turned to Elmer.

"Blue jay," supplied the crew-cut genius. "Adult male."

Sure enough, a bright blue bundle of feathers flashed briefly out of the trees, then just as quickly disappeared.

"See?" laughed Boots. "He's always right."

* * *

Miss Scrimmage screeched the van to a halt diagonally across Route 60. "I can't turn left here!" she exclaimed, staring in consternation at her directions. "That's a dirt road! Catherine, are you sure the man at the gas station said this was the right way?"

Cathy nodded positively. "This is it."

The Headmistress was totally distressed. "But Montreal is a

large city with buildings and people and delightful little shops where they serve butter croissants! Where are they?"

"Maybe they're at the other end of this road," Diane suggested.

"Maybe," said Miss Scrimmage dubiously. But she was terribly upset. And as the road became bumpier and muddier, her agitation grew. "We're lost! Oh, my stars!" She stared at her typed directions, ransacking her mind for a missed turn, a wrong highway number, a left where a right had been called for — anything that would indicate where Montreal might be.

For twenty minutes of jouncing through ruts, she agonized in total confusion as the situation got worse until, with a screech of brakes, she stopped at the end of the road, totally distraught.

"Oh, girls!" the Headmistress whimpered. "This is a terrible dilemma! I'm in a quandary!" She turned back to face them and cried out in astonishment. The five members of the Baking Club were gone, leaving nothing but empty suitcases and discarded blouses and skirts. The girls stood beside the van, dressed in jeans and warm jackets, lacing their boots and shouldering their duffels.

The Headmistress was dazed. "Girls! Girls! Why are you dressed like that? Come back! This isn't Montreal!"

"Surprise!" chorused the five. Miss Scrimmage just gawked.

Cathy handed over a large silver-wrapped package, festooned with ribbons. "Miss Scrimmage," she chided gently, "did you honestly think you could reach fifty years of teaching without us doing something special?"

Bewildered behind the wheel of the van, Miss Scrimmage was suddenly all smiles. "I don't deserve you girls!" she exclaimed emotionally. "Oh, this is so exciting!" She tore at the paper to reveal a gift box from a store called "The Outdoorsman." Inside were hiking boots, jeans and a heavy wool cable-knit sweater.

Miss Scrimmage was even more confused than before. "This is — uh — exactly what I needed," she stammered.

The girls all cheered.

"Try them on, Miss Scrimmage!" crowed Wilma Dorf.

"Oh, yes!" cried Cathy. "You haven't even heard the best part yet! We're taking you on a camping trip!"

The Headmistress was thunderstruck. "But — but — what about the shops with the butter croissants?"

Five faces fell. Eyes became misty. Lower lips trembled.

Cathy spoke up, voice shaky. "We thought it would be a happy surprise for you, Miss Scrimmage. Don't you like it?"

If there was one thing Miss Scrimmage couldn't bear, it was the sight of her girls in any kind of distress.

"I love it!" she said without reservation. "You're all the *dearest* things! Now just let me step into the van to change into my new wardrobe, and we'll be ready to start off on our happy adventure."

Ten minutes later, looking surprisingly youthful and spry in her stylish jeans and sweater, Miss Scrimmage led, or thought she led, the Baking Club into the woods of Algonquin Park. Touched that her girls would go to such lengths to do her honour, Montreal and butter croissants were the last thing on her mind.

* * *

". . . and to make a long story short, I quit taxidermy school and became a talent manager."

The "short" story had taken place over the last three hundred kilometres. Now the blue Ford was heading northeast on Route 60, past the main town, into the heart of Algonquin Park.

Mr. Sturgeon had tuned Goose Golden out hours ago and was concentrating with some alarm on his rearview mirror. It seemed like the same line of cars had been behind him for the whole trip. Surely everyone wasn't going to Algonquin Park. It didn't make sense. No one had turned off anywhere else; no one had passed him. It was as though he were being followed.

Rounding a wide curve, he suddenly recognized one of the vehicles. Four cars back, sitting tall and hunched over the steering wheel, was that red-headed reporter in his Volkswagen. It all made sense. When the Headmaster of Macdonald Hall and Jordie Jones's manager had driven off together early in the morning, and obviously in a big hurry, some of the media people had gambled that the real story lay at their destination. The Ford had picked up — he counted rapidly — eight tails. He had not avoided the circus; he had taken it on the road. Now the wilderness survival trip would be subjected to even more disruption.

"There are reporters following us," Mr. Sturgeon announced with distaste.

Golden looked back in alarm. "Oh, no! Seth isn't going to like this!"

"Well, he's bound to understand how it happened," said the Headmaster reasonably. "And when he hears that you and I left this morning, he'll put two and two together and realize that we've set out to Algonquin Park to bring back Jones."

There was a long silence, then, "He might not know that," said Golden in a strangled voice.

Mr. Sturgeon glanced at him sharply. "You *did* tell him that Jones is with my boys?"

The manager flushed. "Well, I was *going* to — but I kind of fell asleep."

The Headmaster was livid. "Do you mean to tell me Dinkman still thinks Jones is missing?"

Golden shrugged. "Only inasmuch as he doesn't know where he is."

"Spare me your Hollywood doubletalk. You're going to call and explain exactly where we are and what we're doing."

But Dinkman wasn't answering his cell phone, and the film company's line was perpetually busy — probably with incoming inquiries about Jordie's disappearance. As they approached the wilderness of Algonquin Park, the cellular signal faded to zero and the Headmaster gave up. Soon they came to the dirt road, and the Ford was jouncing along, its worn shocks protesting each bump and trough. Then, just as Golden pronounced himself officially carsick, the road ended.

The Headmaster stared in perplexity at the red minivan parked there on the grass. "If I didn't know better," he mused aloud, "I'd swear that was Miss Scrimmage's vehicle." He opened his door. "Come along, Golden. If we hurry, maybe we can lose the reporters in the woods."

No sooner was the manager out of the car than he planted one pristine white doeskin loafer into a mud puddle, which sucked his foot in up to the ankle.

Mr. Sturgeon smiled in grim amusement. "Welcome to Die-in-the-Woods."

* * *

Seth Dinkman stormed across the Macdonald Hall campus to the south lawn, glowering with rage. A radio reporter with a portable tape recorder leapt out at him from the bushes.

"Do you have a comment on the Jordie Jones case, Mr. Dinkman?"

"Yeah! Mind your own business!" roared the director. He grabbed the tape recorder, hurled it twenty metres away into a flower bed and marched on. The crew had been forced to shut down filming because of the swarm of reporters. The phone lines were tied up with media calls, so that even if Jordie were trying to get through, his only response would be a recorded message. Goose had disappeared off the face of the earth. And now Sturgeon was not in his office, and no one had seen him all day. Dinkman was going to get to the bottom of this if he had to tear the campus apart.

He leapt onto the Headmaster's front porch and pounded on the door.

Mrs. Sturgeon answered it. "Good afternoon, Mr. Dinkman. What can I do for you?"

"Hi. Is your husband home?"

"Why, no," she replied. "He's driven up to get Jordie."

"What? *Where's* Jordie?"

"Don't you know? He seems to have joined a group of our boys on a wilderness survival trip."

Dinkman reached up and grabbed two handfuls of his hair. "How come the *director* is the last to know? I've been worrying myself sick over that rotten kid, keeping Goose from falling to pieces, lying my head off to every reporter in town — and it's 'Hey, don't tell Seth! He's *only* in charge of the whole project! What does *he* need to know for?'"

Mrs. Sturgeon clucked sympathetically. "Let me make you a cup of tea."

"No time!" roared Dinkman. "Where are they?"

She shrugged helplessly. "The campsite is in Algonquin Park, just north of the main highway, on one of the little lakes. William knows which one it is this year, but I'm afraid I don't. Please come in and I'll show you the general area on a map."

"Algonquin Park — north of the highway — little lake," the director repeated. "I'll find it. just tell me — where's the closest place I can charter a helicopter?"

* * *

The Baking Club trip to Montreal/Fifty Years of Teaching camping celebration slogged happily through the underbrush, Miss Scrimmage still in the lead.

"Girls, I feel twenty years younger!" the Headmistress gushed, hopping athletically over a large exposed root. "This is ever so much better than a trip to Montreal! The fresh air, the physical challenge, nature all around us, why, even these clothes! I can't remember ever being so comfortable!"

The girls exchanged hilarious glances. Cathy had known they'd be able to manoeuvre her up to Algonquin Park, and even entice her into the woods, but no one had expected her to be so thrilled about it. It was a bonus. For all her craziness, Miss Scrimmage was popular among her students, so everyone was pleased that she was having such a good time.

"How much longer before we get to Jordie?" whispered Diane.

"That depends on how lucky we are," Cathy replied. "They're

camping at the lake just north of here. Once we hit water, we have to circle around until we find their campsite. It could be an hour; it could be three."

"It's worth it!" decided Ruth Sidwell, nodding fervently. "I can't believe we're going to meet Jordie Jones! I mean, we sort of met him at the dance, but that doesn't count because he was disguised as that prince guy."

"And the dance was too crowded and too hectic," added Vanessa Robinson. "This time it'll be a small group." She looked nervous. "What are we going to say when we see him?"

Cathy laughed delightedly. "I don't know about you guys, but I'm going to say, and I quote — " She brought her fists together in front of her and emitted an earsplitting, bloodcurdling, bone-chilling shriek that echoed through the woods in all directions.

"Catherine!" exclaimed Miss Scrimmage in horror. "That is definitely not ladylike!"

"Sorry, Miss Scrimmage," said Cathy. "It's just that every time I hear the name Jordie Jones, I kind of freak out."

"Good gracious," the Headmistress sniffed. "One would think that, if you're fond of a young man, you wouldn't want to frighten him to death by screaming his head off."

"Pssst," whispered Diane. "Jordie Jones."

It tore an identical screech from Cathy's throat.

* * *

"Okay, Elm," said Bruno, "how about that one?" He was referring to a distant cry that could just barely be heard over the sounds of the forest.

Elmer was pop-eyed behind his glasses. Slowly he stood up.

"No," he said finally. "I must be mistaken."

"Come on," said Jordie. "Let's have it."

Elmer flushed. "It was very faint, and I only heard it for a second."

"Ha!" crowed Jordie. "We finally stumped you."

"Hey, Elm," said Bruno. "You're slipping."

"I hope so," said Elmer cryptically.

They were interrupted by Wilbur's bellow from the waterfront: "Somebody's pretty stupid!"

It awoke the snoozing Coach Flynn, who propped himself up on his elbows and called, "Walton, you want to check that out?"

Bruno, Boots and Jordie ran to the slope and peered down to where Wilbur and his crew were attempting to launch the S.S. *Drown-in-the-Woods II*. It was instantly clear what the excitement was about. The raft sat in shallow water. The red underwear letters so painstakingly cut out and glued to the logs read:

H E E P

Bruno and Boots turned to each other. "I thought *you* were making the L," they said at exactly the same time.

"No one's going to rescue us with this," said Pete sadly.

"Why?" asked Larry. "Don't the illiterate deserve to be saved?"

"Well, what if they rescue us and then dock us on our English grade?"

"I don't take English, remember?" grinned Mark.

Wilbur bunched both fists. "If you don't stop filming this raft, that video camera is going to the bottom of the lake, and you're going with it!"

"Just trim the stupid E," called Bruno.

In the distance, another fierce screech sounded, a little louder this time.

The three turned to regard Elmer. Macdonald Hall's top student had heard it too. He stood stiff as a pointer, nostrils flared, eyes haunted.

Boots cocked an eyebrow. "I wonder what it is."

Chapter 15

Is it Dangerous?

Goose Golden slumped down on a rock and passed a grubby hand over his scratched face. "I'm not going to make it!" he rasped hoarsely. "You go on without me! Tell J.J. I tried!"

Mr. Sturgeon uncorked a canteen and handed it to his companion. "Enough melodrama. You are here at your own insistence, over my protest, and you will take your medicine like a man."

Golden shivered. His light linen sports clothes were no match for the damp chill of the north woods. "It's your fault! You said this was a park! A park is swings, a few trees, grass, benches, maybe a baseball diamond. This is the Amazon rain forest!"

"It's the wilderness survival trip," the Headmaster explained. "We prefer not to have it in the grand ballroom of the Waldorf Astoria."

He regarded the manager in some amusement. What had formerly been a white, stylish, California-tailored outfit was now good only for the ragpicker. Mud, grass stains and the juice of countless rotted berries dotted the white linen everywhere. Golden had spent more time flat on his face than on his feet, and he looked it.

"Come along, Golden. We're losing time here. Those reporters can't be far behind us."

The manager wasn't budging. "What a place to bring a bunch of kids! What have you got against Disneyland? This is the hairy armpit of the universe! It's freezing, it's dangerous, it's filthy, it stinks and it's full of *animals*!" There was a scream in the distance. "See? Now, what makes a sound like that? I don't know, but I sure wouldn't invite it up to the house for a barbecue!"

Mr. Sturgeon frowned. He had noticed the sounds as well, and had never heard anything quite like it in the woods before. He grabbed Golden and hauled him to his feet. Suddenly he had an urgent desire to see his boys safe and sound.

* * *

The screams were getting louder. Elmer sat on a log in the middle of camp, staring at the surrounding woods, his face grey. The other campers were clustered around the tents, murmuring nervously among themselves.

"Gee," said Pete. "Elmer looks pretty scared. It must be something real nasty."

"Nonsense," said the coach. "He's just bewildered because he doesn't know what it is." He looked around at the frightened faces of his students. "This has gone far enough. Drimsdale, come over here." Elmer presented himself. "What's going on? Do you have any idea what's making that noise?"

Elmer stared at him. "Sir, do we have any weapons?"

Flynn gawked. "Just our Swiss Army knives. Why?"

"I was thinking more along the lines of a high-powered tranquilizer rifle."

"All right, Drimsdale," ordered Flynn. "Speak up. What's out there?"

Elmer swallowed hard. "*Panthera carnivora*. The spotted tundra leopard."

"What is it?" asked Boots anxiously.

"Well," said Elmer thoughtfully, "it's three metres long, with a powerful set of jaws that apply pressure equivalent to a two-tonne hydraulic press. The teeth are razor-sharp and elongated for flesh ripping. Its habitat is usually the northern tundra, and it feeds primarily upon sea lions, walruses, caribou, polar bears, musk oxen, beached whales, un-spotted tundra leopards and, occasionally, man."

"Is it dangerous?" asked Pete.

"What kind of stupid question is that?" cried Wilbur. "Does it *sound* harmless?"

An echoing shriek from the woods was his answer.

"But this isn't the tundra," protested Larry.

"That's what had me confused at first," was Elmer's reply. "But now that I'm convinced we're dealing with an actual *Panthera carnivora*, we can only conclude that the food supply ran low in northern latitudes, and it's come south — " he shuddered, "— to feed."

"In other words," said Bruno miserably, "he already ate everybody in the tundra, and now he's coming here to eat us."

"Enough!" interrupted Coach Flynn. "Look, boys, I'm Ontario born and bred, and when I was younger, I camped in Algonquin Park every year. They've got bears here, maybe a few wolves, lots of rodents and some birds. That's it. No offence, Drimsdale, but this time you're wrong."

Elmer hung his head. "I only wish I were, sir."

There was another scream from whatever it was.

"Oh, this is ridiculous!" exclaimed the coach. "Look at you! You're acting like a bunch of babies! Who do you believe — Drimsdale or me?"

This was followed by an uncomfortable silence.

"You know," said Mark finally, "I've still got some video-tape. Maybe we should each record a last message to our folks. Just in case."

"Are you kidding?" roared Calvin. "I'm going to make that leopard wish he'd never left the tundra! I'm going to rip off his spots and shove them down his throat! I'm going to tear him limb from limb!" His voice broke. "I'm going to tell my mother, and she'll sue Macdonald Hall for every cent they've got! I'm too young to die! Oh, man! Oh, man!"

"I can't believe this!" howled Flynn. "Would you just cut it out! Nobody's going to eat anybody — " He was interrupted by the next shriek, which was louder and a lot closer. It lifted everybody ten centimetres off the ground.

Chaos ensued. In spite of Coach Flynn's protests, the boys began to run around aimlessly. There was nowhere to go, but they felt better moving.

"It's almost here!"

"It's coming from the west!"

"Prepare to defend yourselves!"

"It's coming from the north!"

"Get a big stick!"

"It's coming from the east!"

Bruno rummaged madly through his duffel, pulling out his Swiss Army knife. "Oh, great!" he cried out in exasperation. "The blade's broken! All I've got is the can opener! Can you just see me fighting off a leopard with a can opener?"

Boots, brandishing a cast-iron frying pan, handed Bruno a pot to use as a weapon. The exchange brought them to a halt, and they stood frozen in time for a few seconds, staring at each other. Neither spoke, but the question was obvious. Was this the end?

"Nah!" Bruno snapped back to life first. He looked around. "Hey, Elm, can these tundra leopards swim?"

"Of course not," replied Elmer. "All cats avoid water."

Bruno threw his arms up in exasperation. "Well, get with the program, guys! We spent all day yesterday building a *raft*!"

For a second, all activity ceased in the campsite. Then there was a mad dash for the lakefront. Wilbur and Larry picked up Coach Flynn and ran him battering ram style for the slope.

"Stop!" bellowed Flynn.

Everyone froze.

"Aren't we forgetting something here?" the coach demanded, hanging horizontal in the arms of the two boys. *"I'm* the teacher! You do what *I* say!"

The loudest shriek of them all cut through the clearing, followed by a sound even more terrifying — a rustling in the bushes. Something was very, very close.

"Everybody onto the raft!" howled Flynn.

They stampeded down the hill, bearing their teacher.

The rustling grew louder, then the bushes parted. Into the

now-deserted clearing stepped William R. Sturgeon, Headmaster of Macdonald Hall.

"This is the campsite," he called over his shoulder. "I told you I heard voices."

Goose Golden's eyes peered out from behind two broad green leaves. "Is it safe to come out? That animal sounds really close!"

"Flynn? Fudge?" called the Headmaster. There was no answer, and no one in sight.

At the lake, Wilbur hauled in the last length of rope that brought the raft to shore.

"What if it won't support all of us?" asked Jordie.

Boots stared at him. "You want to stay here while we find out?"

They clambered aboard, with Coach Flynn lying on his side and everyone else standing up. Wilbur pushed the raft away from the bank, jumping on it as it moved off. The craft pitched dangerously and then stabilized. Everyone cheered, including the teacher.

"Yo, leopard!" cried Bruno exuberantly. "Do your worst!"

"Hah!" snarled Calvin. "You should have let me at him, Coach! I'd have ripped his head off!"

"Next time, Fihzgart."

As they slowly drifted out, Larry pointed up the hill toward the campsite. "Hey!" he said in confusion. "There's a *guy* up there!"

All eyes turned to the figure at the top of the slope. "What are you, crazy, mister?" called Bruno. "Get down here! We'll save you!"

Boots, known for his keen eyesight, squinted at the man. "It's The Fish!" he gasped.

"It can't be!" said Bruno. "Where's his suit?"

"Did you find anything?" called a voice from behind Mr. Sturgeon.

Jordie perked up in sudden recognition. "*Goose!*" he cried. "It's me, Jordie!"

"*J.J.!*" The tattered figure of Goose Golden appeared over the hill in a full sprint. He was running so fast that his weary body outpaced his stumbling feet. Down the slope he went, tumbling head over heels.

Mr. Sturgeon started after him, stepping carefully.

"It's not him," whispered Bruno to Boots. "The Fish would never wear a dumb hat like that."

"Mr. Sturgeon! Mr. Golden!" called Elmer urgently. "Quick! Come onto the raft! There is a spotted tundra leopard stalking us!"

The Headmaster helped Golden to his feet. "A spotted tundra leopard? You must be mistaken, Drimsdale."

A deafening, terrifying shriek came from above them.

"Oh, sir," pleaded Elmer, "it's in the camp, and it's coming this way! You're in grave danger!"

Mr. Sturgeon was perplexed. "It's illogical, Drimsdale. I have no idea what that sound is, but it is *not* a tundra leopard two thousand kilometres off course!"

Another savage cry, the loudest and fiercest of them all, echoed menacingly over the lake.

Instantly, the Headmaster was into the water and running. Knees pumping high, he splashed through the shallows out to the raft, where willing hands hauled him aboard. Goose Golden was hot on his heels.

Twelve people hunched on the bobbing S.S. *Drown-in-the-Woods II*, their eyes fixed on the hill, waiting for the deadly cat to appear.

There was another shriek, and another and then the source of all that ferocious sound came screaming over the crest of the hill and stood silhouetted in the late afternoon sun.

Cathy Burton.

"Cathy?!" chorused Bruno and Boots in disbelief.

Elmer was chagrined. "Perhaps I made a slight miscalculation."

Mr. Sturgeon glared at him. "Understatement, Drimsdale."

Cathy stared down at them. "What's everybody doing out there? Didn't anyone ever tell you not to overload a boat?" She waved and added, "Hi, Jordie."

Weakly, the star waved back.

Miss Scrimmage puttered up to Cathy. "I just saw the most adorable little bunny rabbit!" She stared at the raft, then broke into a tremulous smile. "Oh, Catherine, the gifts and the camping trip were really more than enough! But to bring a barge with all my friends so we could have a party" — she dabbed at the corner of her eye with a lace handkerchief — "I don't know what to say!"

Diane and the other three girls rushed onto the scene. "Is he there?" They took in the sight of the jam-packed raft and fell silent.

The unmistakable clatter of rotor blades was heard. All eyes turned skyward. A small bubble helicopter appeared in the bright sky, hovered briefly and began to descend.

"Man!" exclaimed Pete in disgust. "Somebody finally flies right over the lake, and he can't read our HELP sign 'cause we're all standing on it!"

As the craft descended, Jordie squinted up at it. "It's Seth!"

The director's head and megaphone emerged from the bubble. *"Is Jordie down there?"* rang through the woods.

Careful not to upset the raft, Bruno and Boots inched aside so the director could see his star. Jordie waved. An amplified sigh of relief skimmed the treetops.

Golden signalled madly, windmilling his arms so violently that the platform began to bob, soaking Coach Flynn from head to toe. "I'm here, too, Seth! Don't worry! I'm okay!"

The helicopter moved directly over the manager, and the sudden gust of wind from the blades lifted the toupee clean off his head. The hairpiece was carried out to the centre of the lake. Just as it was about to settle down onto the water, an enormous grey muskie broke the surface, snapped up its prize and disappeared with a splash into the depths.

The laughter that rang out through the megaphone was positively diabolical. *"Okay, everybody gets a lift home except Goose!"*

There was a click, and Mark Davies lowered his camera and heaved a contented sigh. "Out of tape! But man, what a documentary!"

Mr. Sturgeon turned very gingerly, and looked into every face on the raft. "I say — where's Fudge?"

Coach Flynn's jaw dropped. "I thought it was Fudge that sent *you*!"

The Headmaster threw his hands up in exasperation. "What a miserable muddle! Fudge gone, the trip ruined, my athletic director injured and all of us packed like sardines on this raft, looking proper idiots, stranded in the middle of nowhere! It could not possibly be more humiliating!"

No sooner were the words out of his mouth than eight reporters exploded over the crest of the hill, cameras clicking.

Mr. Sturgeon held his head. "I stand corrected."

By this time, the Baking Club had hold of the rope and was hauling the S.S. *Drown-in-the-Woods II* to shore.

Wilbur checked his watch. "Gee," he said, "I hope we don't get back to school in time for dinner." He shuddered. "It's fish night."

Chapter 16

The Super-Duper Jumbo-Boomer

It was the last day of filming and, as a tribute to his hosts, Seth Dinkman was making it something of an occasion. Only two scenes remained to be done at Macdonald Hall — the grand finale, which was the explosion of the miniature Faculty Building and the re-shooting of the stunt Bruno had hijacked on the eve of Die-in-the-Woods. Figuring that nothing else could possibly go wrong, Dinkman had thrown the set open to both schools, and most of the reporters tracking Jordie Jones were there, too.

Miss Scrimmage, once again wearing her sweater, jeans and hiking boots, stood with the Sturgeons, proudly watching as the star mingled politely with her students, shaking hands and signing autograph books. Headmaster and Headmistress had settled their differences, and all lawsuits were dropped. Macdonald Hall had agreed to buy Miss Scrimmage another shotgun.

Only Goose Golden was absent. While waiting to be airlifted out of the woods, he had sustained a severe sunburn on the top of his bald head and was recovering in Jordie's trailer.

Cathy and Diane had separated themselves from the crowd

of girls surrounding the teen idol and were standing with Bruno and Boots.

Cathy watched her fellow students with tolerant amusement. "Can you believe those girls, drooling over Jordie like that?"

Boots stared at her. "*Yeah*, I can believe it! Two minutes ago it was *you*, not only drooling, but dragging poor Miss Scrimmage halfway across the province and screaming the woods down!"

"The point is," Cathy continued, "sure, it's great to meet a movie star. But once the mystery is gone, it's no big deal. I mean, Jordie's a nice guy, but he's just a guy. The glamour is strictly on the screen."

"I'll tell Cutesy," said Bruno coldly. "He'll be so thrilled to know he's nothing special."

"Okay," flushed Diane. "So we went a little overboard. But you two were just as bad, getting so mad about it."

Bruno didn't smile. "Just call it one of those babyish reactions you have when your best friends blow you off like you didn't exist."

"Well, you didn't have to get all jealous," said Cathy. "You know a million movie stars couldn't replace you guys."

Bruno and Boots looked at each other.

"Okay," said Bruno finally, "I think they've grovelled enough."

"You're off the hook," grinned Boots. "But you owe us."

"Plus Elmer Drimsdale needs a favour," added Bruno. "He wants you to help him make a tape of different wildcat sounds. He'd ask you himself, but he's in his room reading up on the spotted tundra leopard."

"Shhh!" hissed Mark, steadying his reloaded video camera. "Mr. Dinkman's ready to talk." Mr. Sturgeon had given Mark permission to record one last day of filming, provided he promised never to touch another video cassette until summer.

"Okay, sports fans," called Dinkman into the megaphone. *"This is the home stretch. We blow up the school, we re-shoot the busting water pipe stunt and we're on the plane to L.A. So let's get it right. The school comes first. Flag me when the explosives are hooked up."*

A short distance away, two special-effects technicians were running wires from their detonating plunger to the hidden cable that led to the carefully placed charges inside the Faculty Building model. One of the electricians reached down and pulled the end of an insulated wire that was partially buried in a flower bed.

"Here she is. Hook 'er up."

His colleague frowned. "Are you sure we ran the cable all the way over here? It's twenty metres to the model."

"Maybe we don't want the plunger on camera, jerk. Just do it."

Reluctantly the second man made the connection. "We'd be off-screen if we were ten metres closer, and you know the big push to save equipment expenses," he said, still doubtful. "We'd better check with Seth. Maybe we're hooking up the wrong thing."

The first technician laughed. "This is a school. They don't have low-impedance detonator cable sticking up out of every flower bed!" He took off his hat and waved it at the director. "All ready, Seth!"

But the technician was mistaken. There was one other low-impedance detonator cable on campus. It was the wire Elmer Drimsdale had stretched around Jordie Jones's trailer to set off the fireworks attack. That had been the night when Jordie had started off as the enemy and ended up a new friend. The boys had removed all the fireworks — all except one piece. The Super-Duper Jumbo-Boomer still lurked there, half buried, pointing up at the trailer. Its wick was attached to a length of low-impedance detonator cable buried in a flower bed and now hooked up to Seth Dinkman's plunger.

"Okay! Action!"

Four cameras, focused at various angles on the miniature Faculty Building, started rolling. The director raised his arm, then dropped it in signal. The special effects technicians pushed the plunger. Hundreds of pairs of eyes were riveted on the model.

Nothing happened.

Dinkman stared in disbelief at his final scene. Where was the explosion? Where was the fire? He turned a furious countenance to his special effects team. *"Push the stupid plunger!"*

"We did, boss!"

Boots heard it first — a sputtering, hissing sound behind them. He wheeled. There was smoke coming from underneath Jordie's trailer. And sparks. He tapped his roommate on the shoulder. "Hey, Bruno — "

WHOOSH!!!

The Super-Duper Jumbo-Boomer launched out of its hole like a missile from a silo. It deflected off the undercarriage of the trailer, sheared off both emergency brakes and shot out from under the camper, heading for the crowd. Spectators dove in all directions as the big rocket screeched through their ranks, a metre off the ground. Then it turned upwards and roared off into the sky, leaving a trail of sparks.

BOOM!!!

The explosion rocked the countryside. Showers of coloured light rained down on everyone. The crowd *ooh*-ed and *aah*-ed, and some even applauded.

"Hey," said Cathy, mildly annoyed. "That was my Super-Duper Jumbo-Boomer. You guys owe me one Super-Duper Jumbo-Boomer."

Bruno and Boots didn't hear her. They were staring in horror at the big trailer with the star on the door. Its emergency brakes gone, there was nothing anchoring it to the uneven ground. It began to roll, very slowly at first, then picking up speed as the campus sloped downwards to the lower-lying north lawn.

Goose Golden's sunburned bald head poked out the window. "Hey! What's going on?"

"Hit the brakes!" screamed Bruno.

Like a juggernaut, the runaway trailer bowled along, bearing down on the film crew. They scattered like tenpins. Even Seth Dinkman had to make a desperate dive to safety.

"Heeeelp!" cried Goose.

The camper sailed harmlessly past the cameras, which were still dutifully rolling. It missed the light reflectors and sound equipment, too. Gaining momentum, it barrelled through the heart of the set and ploughed over the model of the Macdonald Hall Faculty Building, crushing it into splinters. Then it continued onto level ground and stopped.

Dinkman had his hands over his face. "It didn't happen! It didn't happen!" He uncovered his eyes. "It happened."

Miss Scrimmage was looking on in perplexity. "A building being run over by a giant trailer! What a strange movie!"

The general chaos was enhanced by the arrival of a yellow taxicab along the road that led from the main driveway. The rear door opened and out stepped Mr. Fudge, still in full camping attire.

The Housemaster cupped his hands to his mouth and called, "Can anyone lend me three hundred and forty-seven dollars and fifty cents?"

Seth Dinkman sat on the grass, his head in his hands, his crew gathered around him, awaiting orders. "This place is jinxed. Forget the model. We'll build another one in California."

"What about the stunt?" asked a cameraman. Dinkman made a face. "Let's get it over with. Where's Charlie?"

"Waiting for the ambulance."

"What?"

A production assistant provided the explanation. "He threw his back out dodging the camper. Should we send for another stuntman?"

The director flushed bright purple. "No! I refuse to spend five more seconds in this — this *war zone*! We filmed a perfectly good stunt last week, and I intend to use it!"

"We've been over that," said the assistant. "The kid's not in the union."

"Yeah?" roared Dinkman. "Well, I'm going to call in every favour I have in the world, lie, cheat, bribe, threaten and *get* him in the union!" He looked up to see Bruno standing nearby, hope written all over his face. "Yeah, kid, you heard right. Congratulations. You're in the movie."

With a shriek of pure joy, Bruno hurled himself straight into the air, pumping his fists in ecstasy. By the time he came back to earth, Boots and Jordie had joined his celebration, thrilled that, after all his efforts and near misses, their friend had finally made it into *Academy Blues*. The three stood there, laughing, cheering and pounding each other on the back.

Boots was almost hysterical. "I can't believe you actually made it!"

Bruno looked offended. "I never doubted it for a second." Abruptly his face fell. "Hey, Cutesy — this means the filming's over! You're leaving today!"

Jordie nodded solemnly then broke into a big grin. "But guess what? The world premiere is going to be in Toronto! I'm coming back!"

There was more celebrating.

"And I want you guys to be my special guests at the big opening," Jordie went on.

Bruno's face was glowing pink with pleasure. "I'll probably have to sign a few autographs myself," he said thoughtfully. "I'm the stuntman. This is my first step on the road to superstardom!"

And suddenly he was making his way through the crowd, waving frantically at the director.

"Hey, Mr. Dinkman — is this a good time to discuss salary . . . ?

Epilogue

Sir Michael Markham was the toughest critic in Hollywood. He yawned his way through the most exciting action films ever made. Comedies that had viewers howling hysterically in the aisles put him to sleep. While audiences dabbed at their eyes during heartwrenching tearjerkers, he was beset by giggles. And as star-crossed lovers kissed passionately on the screen, Sir Michael sat in the front row, crunching extra-thick potato chips so loudly that the sound carried all the way to the rear of the theatre.

So, at the Toronto premiere of *Academy Blues*, after all the other critics had pronounced the movie another Jordie Jones success, there was an expectant pause when the question was posed to Markham.

It was a one-word review. Sir Michael simply said, "Fertilizer."

"He must have loved it," was Seth Dinkman's opinion. Everyone expected negatives from Markham, so none of the cast, crew or producers was heartbroken.

Except for one stuntman. "The nerve of that guy!" raged

Bruno, once again resplendent in the red velvet jacket he had worn on the first day of *Academy Blues*. "Dumping on *our movie*! I'll fertilize *him*!"

"Don't worry about it," Jordie assured him. "Sir Michael hates everything. He called *Gone With the Wind* a big bomb."

After the premiere, a fleet of limousines whisked the guests off to the Empress Hotel, where Dinkman had rented the Ambassador Suite for a mammoth party. It was there that Bruno, Boots, Elmer, Larry, Sidney, Pete, Wilbur and Mark presented Jordie with a videotape.

"So you'll never forget us," grinned Bruno.

"Fat chance of that!" exclaimed the star fervently. He examined the tape. "What is it?"

"A copy of my documentary," Mark said proudly. "I got an A double-plus."

"And only a C minus on editing," Pete reminded him.

"How could I cut anything out?" Mark demanded righteously. "Everything was perfect!"

All of the suite's eleven TV sets were on, and the boys settled themselves at a corner monitor and popped Mark's tape into the machine.

Switching back and forth from narration to musical soundtrack, the video documented the making of *Academy Blues* in painstaking detail. Everything from the loading and unloading of equipment, the actors rehearsing their lines and the crew having lunch, to the activity in the makeup trailer was included. But what really made Mark's piece fascinating were the extra intercuts between the scenes of Dinkman and Jordie in action. Booby-trapping the trailer, poker night, Mr. Sturgeon dismantling Miss Scrimmage's shotgun, Bruno's flubs as an actor — the boys watched in fascination and awe.

At first they were by themselves in the corner, but soon some of the adults became aware of the video and began to drift over. Those who came stayed, watching with curiosity and interest. Gradually, more and more people gathered around the set. The documentary unfolded — the dance, the hockey game, the press conference, Bruno's stunt and the rapid-fire disasters of Die-in-the-Woods, starring Cathy Burton as the spotted tundra leopard.

Then came the credits — directed by Mark Davies, produced by Mark Davies, edited by Mark Davies, concept by Mark Davies, based on an original idea by Mark Davies — all super-imposed over the image of the Macdonald Hall Faculty Building being run over by Jordie Jones's trailer.

By this time, all eyes in the Ambassador Suite — actors', crew members', critics' and guests' — were riveted to the screen. No one spoke. No one even moved. For a moment, you could hear a pin drop. Mark's video on the making of *Academy Blues* had left a hundred and fifty people, most of them film professionals, completely speechless.

The silence was broken by applause, not from a crowd, but from one person. Heads turned in all directions to locate its source. There at the back of the group, face pink with pleasure, clapping his heart out, stood Sir Michael Markham. "Bravo!" he called. *"Bravo!"*

No one could believe it. The toughest critic in Hollywood, the sourpuss of Sunset Boulevard, the man who hated every-thing, *liked* — no, *loved* — no, was absolutely *crazy* about Mark's video.

Seth Dinkman began to clap, too, followed by Jordie, the crew and Goose Golden. Bruno and Boots joined in, then the rest of the boys and finally all the guests, a hundred and fifty strong, burst into thunderous applause. Glowing, Mark took a bow, overjoyed by his ovation.

"He's hated everything that's come out of Hollywood in fifty years," said Dinkman as soon as the cheers had died down, "and *this* he likes!"

Bruno looked at the director, an enormous grin splitting his face. "For action, adventure and real-life drama," he said, "you just can't beat Macdonald Hall!"

Be sure to read the next
hilarious Macdonald Hall
adventure:

The JOKE'S
on US

Chapter 1

Over the Hill

"Take my word for it, Bruno — you're not going to like him."

The speaker was Boots O'Neal. He and Bruno Walton, his longtime roommate and friend, were hanging movie posters on the walls of room 306 of Macdonald Hall.

Bruno spat out a thumbtack. "Of course I'll like him. You're just saying that because he's your brother."

"No, I'm not."

"Yes, you are," Bruno insisted. "I mean, look at me. I hate my sister, and everybody else says she's the sweetest kid on earth. It's human nature."

"You don't know Edward," Boots said flatly.

"Sure I do!"

"You've only met him twice. And he was on his best behaviour because it was vacation and my folks were around. The kid is crazy!"

"He's totally normal," Bruno countered. He took a step back to admire the new decor. "I think this one's a little crooked."

"It's fine," Boots retorted. "Dormitory 3 is crooked."

Bruno slipped into the shoe he'd been using as a hammer. He

213

breathed deeply. "I envy your brother — young, new, first year at Macdonald Hall — he's got his whole life ahead of him."

Boots had to laugh. "And we're grandfathers, I suppose?"

"We have so much to teach him," Bruno raved on. "We can show him the ropes."

"Oh, sure," said Boots sarcastically. "He should really listen to us. We've been in trouble more than any two guys in the history of the Hall. We've washed more dishes, picked up more garbage, raked more leaves and shovelled more snow. And we definitely hold the record for being chewed out by the Fish."

"The Fish," said Bruno, smiling at the mere thought of William R. Sturgeon, the Headmaster. "Your brother hasn't even met the Fish yet! Were we ever that young?"

"Yes, we were," growled Boots. "It was a better life."

Bruno looked annoyed. "Your problem, Melvin, is that you're a crab. As soon as new student orientation is over, Edward will drop by here, the three of us will get along great and all your whining and complaining will be for nothing."

The words were barely out of his mouth when the door flew open, and there stood Edward O'Neal. He looked very much like a younger version of Boots — blond, blue-eyed, with a sleek, athletic build.

"Eddie!" Bruno greeted the newcomer. "How's it going? Remember me? Bruno?" He bounded over and dealt Boots's brother a hearty slap on the back.

Edward's blue eyes crossed and rolled back in his head. Without a sound, he crumpled to the floor and lay there, unmoving.

Bruno stared, bug-eyed. "What did I do? What happened? I didn't hit him that hard! Call Nurse Hildegarde! Dial 911! . . ."

"Bruno — " Boots began patiently.

"We've got to keep him warm till the ambulance comes!" Bruno howled hysterically. "Quick, get a blanket!"

From the floor, Edward reached up, pulled the top sheet from Boots's bed and handed it to Bruno. "Thanks!" gasped Bruno, covering up the victim. He froze. "Hey, wait a minute — "

Edward rose to his feet, dusting himself off.

Boots grimaced. "Come on, Edward. Why do you have to pull that weird stuff on the first day?"

Edward regarded the dumbfounded Bruno. "I'm waiting for the fun to start. The laugh-a-minute thrills. The topsy-turvy roller coaster of excitement."

Bruno found his voice at last. "*What*?"

"For half my life, every phone call, every letter home, was full of 'Bruno says,' and 'Bruno did,' and how great and how cool it was to be at Macdonald Hall with Bruno," sneered Edward. "Well, here I am, on the spot with the Lord of Coolness himself. And I've got to tell you — I'm not impressed." And he turned on his heel and left.

The stunned silence that followed was broken by Boots's voice. "I told you you weren't going to like him."

* * *

Bruno and Boots crouched in the bushes outside their window, scouting the darkened campus.

"All clear," whispered Bruno.

Keeping low to the ground, they snaked along the edge of

Macdonald Hall property, scampered across the road and scaled the wrought-iron fence that surrounded Miss Scrimmage's Finishing School for Young Ladies.

Bruno picked up a handful of pebbles and tossed them at a second-story window. No response.

Boots frowned. "Didn't Cathy and Diane know we'd be dropping by tonight?"

"Give it a few minutes," Bruno shrugged. "Maybe there's a teacher around, or something."

They retreated to the shadows of Miss Scrimmage's nearby apple orchard and sat down to watch the window and wait.

"You know," said Bruno, "I've been thinking about Eddie."

Boots made a face. "Why? I don't, if I can possibly avoid it. And by the way, it's 'Edward.'"

Bruno nodded. "Yeah. He's a real jerk, and all that, but I understand him. This is his first time away from home. He's probably really scared. And he wants everybody to like him."

"Well, he made a great start today," Boots grunted. "I thought you were going to rip his lungs out."

"He's not so bad," chuckled Bruno. "He'll settle down. We'll introduce him to all the guys. Maybe we'll even bring him over here one night." He glanced at his watch. "Hey, what's keeping the girls?"

Boots stood up. "Maybe we should come back tomorrow."

"Nothing doing. The window's open. We'll wait for them inside." He began to stride toward the building.

Boots followed, listing the reasons why this was a bad idea. "Maybe their room got changed . . . maybe they haven't arrived at school yet . . . maybe Miss Scrimmage is up there with her shotgun — "

But Bruno was already shinnying up the drainpipe. Breathing a silent prayer, Boots started up after him.

Bruno swung a leg over the sill and let himself into the room, helping Boots in behind him.

"Well, they've definitely moved in," said Boots, peering into a closet that was full of clothing. Bruno snapped his fingers. "I've got it. They knew we were coming, and they're raiding the kitchen to put up a big spread. Let's go surprise them."

"Aw, c'mon," moaned Boots. "It's one thing to sneak in here; it's another to go wandering around Scrimmage's in the middle of the night! Let's wait."

But once again, he ended up following Bruno's lead. They navigated the dim, carpeted halls, slid down the bannister of the main staircase and stepped into the ornate dining room. On tiptoe, they made their way among the round tables and paused at the door to the kitchen. There was the sound of muffled laughter and quiet singing.

"See!" said Bruno triumphantly. "I told you they were expecting us. It's a party!"

He booted open the swinging door and prepared to bound inside. He froze.

About twenty girls were assembled, eating sandwiches, drinking soda and singing along with a lone visitor, who was strumming on a ukulele.

Bruno stared. The guest of honour was Edward O'Neal.

Wham! The big door swung back, catching him full in the

face. He staggered away, giving Boots a clear view of the festivities as the door swung the other way.

"*Edward*?"

The two boys ran into the kitchen. Boots's little brother was flanked by Cathy Burton on his right and Diane Grant on his left. On the counter in front of him sat an enormous slab of triple-chocolate cake.

"Hey, dudes," Cathy greeted. "Meet Edward. He's new at the Hall."

"These are the two guys we were telling you about," Diane informed Edward.

Edward regarded them critically. "Come to think of it, I saw them over there in Dormitory 3. They were crocheting doilies."

This got a big laugh from the girls.

"Oh, shut up, Edward!" snapped Boots. "Look, girls, he's my kid brother, okay?"

At this news, Edward did another one of his phoney faints. He rolled off his chair to the floor, dropping his ukulele as he fell. This got a standing ovation from the girls.

"Edward — " said Boots warningly.

Bruno managed a brave smile. "Come on, Boots, back off. All the kid needs is a little patience and understanding."

Edward was on his feet again. "Why don't you two *old men* go home and take a nap? Face it — you're over the hill. It's time for a new generation."

It took Boots, Cathy and Diane to remove Bruno's hands from around Edward's throat.

"Let go of me, Boots!" Bruno ordered. "And prepare to become an only child!"

"Pick on someone your own size, Bruno Walton!" cried Diane in outrage.

Bruno strained forward. "Let me at him!"

Edward made a big show of yawning, then checked his watch. "Well, I guess I'd better call it a night."

"You're not going to bed until after the autopsy!" Bruno roared.

"Don't be such a bully!" snapped Cathy.

"Goodnight, all," Edward called. "Thanks for your hospitality." He took three casual steps, and then broke into a sprint across the dining room.

"Come back here!" Bruno tore free and launched himself in pursuit of the fleeing Edward. Boots and the girls rushed after them.

Footsteps and heavy breathing echoed through the halls, but there were no shouts. No one wanted to wake up Miss Scrimmage and her staff.

Bruno and Boots had been in Miss Scrimmage's school many times and knew the layout by heart. But Edward was lost. Around and around the main floor he went, at the head of the chase. Finally, he spied a back staircase and made a dash for it.

Diane gasped. "That's Miss Scrimmage's suite!" But everyone who heard her already knew that. And the boys were out of earshot, halfway up the stairs.

A diabolical grin appeared on Cathy's face. "This is going to be our best year yet! Who says education can't be exciting?"

The boys reached the second floor and hit the hall running.

They were at top speed when a door opened, and Miss Scrimmage stepped out into their path.

Edward hit the brakes, and stopped dead. Bruno slammed into Edward from behind, and Boots nearly tripped over the two of them. The three froze there, hanging onto each other for support. In his misery, Boots caught sight of Cathy and Diane crouched on the top step. Diane looked petrified; Cathy winked.

"Oh, my goodness," the Headmistress mused, adjusting her hairnet and tightening the belt on her robe. "I can't see a thing without my glasses. Now, where did I put my Cream of Wheat?" She began to feel her way around a small kitchen alcove.

Bruno drew in a shaky breath, about to sneeze. Like lightning, a finger — Edward's — appeared under his nose to stifle the impulse. Boots's sigh of relief shook all three of them.

"Ah, here it is," Miss Scrimmage announced. She started back toward her bedroom. But the spoon slipped off the tray, and landed on the carpet with a soft thud. She bent down and felt around with her free hand. Instead of the spoon, her fingers closed upon the toe of Edward's sneaker.

"*A-choo!*" Bruno's sneeze came out at last.

"*A-a-a-augh!*" shrieked Miss Scrimmage, tossing her tray in the air.

Boots grabbed Bruno with one hand and Edward with the other, and headed for the stairs.

Cathy whispered, "We'll cover for you!" She and Diane ran to their Headmistress, who was screaming and picking Cream of Wheat out of her curlers.

"Oh, Miss Scrimmage! Oh, Miss Scrimmage! You were brilliant!"

The Headmistress stopped shrieking and looked up. "I – I – I – was?"

Cathy nodded earnestly. "The way you threw oatmeal at those burglars and scared them away — you saved us! You're a hero!"

"It was Cream of Wheat, dear," said Miss Scrimmage, resettling herself like a hen on a nest. "And I have some information for you: those were no ordinary burglars. Those were marauders from Macdonald Hall."

"No!" Cathy and Diane pretended disbelief.

"Yes, indeed," the Headmistress confirmed. "And you may believe that Mr. Sturgeon will be hearing from me first thing in the morning!"

* * *

All the way back to Macdonald Hall, Bruno was seething. "So we're old men, eh? Over the hill? Well, tonight two old men saved your butt from Miss Scrimmage!"

Edward was outraged. "Saved *my* butt? I'm not the one who sneezed in her face!"

"But you are the idiot who blundered right into her private hallway!" Bruno accused. "If she'd had her shotgun, we'd all be part of the wall!"

"Stay away from Scrimmage's!" Boots hissed.

Edward raised big innocent eyes. "Like you do?"

"Look," said Bruno. "This is the way it is: out of respect for the O'Neal family, I've decided to let you live. But keep out of my face. And don't you ever call me 'old man' again!"

"Yes, O Aged One," deadpanned Edward, and scampered off to Dormitory 1.

Boots sighed miserably. "So sue me. You can't choose your relatives."

About the Author

GORDON KORMAN'S first book, *This Can't Be Happening at Macdonald Hall!*, was published when he was only fourteen. Since then he has written more than seventy teen and middle-grade novels, including six more books about Macdonald Hall. Favourites include the *New York Times* bestselling *The 39 Clues: Cahills vs. Vespers Book One: The Medusa Plot; Ungifted; Schooled*; and the Hypnotist, Swindle and Island series. Born and raised in Canada, Gordon now lives with his family on Long Island, New York.

This CAN'T Be HAPPENING at Macdonald Hall

Macdonald Hall is a grand old boarding school. But this year there are two students who want to shake things up a little: Bruno Walton and Boots O'Neal. They're roommates and best friends, and they know how to have fun. To Headmaster Sturgeon they're nothing but trouble.

Soon they have to face their worst nightmare — separated, with new roommates. But that won't stop them. Whatever it takes — even skunk stunts and an ant stampede — they'll be together again by the end of the semester.

And this is only the beginning.

ISBN 978-0-545-28924-5

Go JUMP in the POOL

For the students of Macdonald Hall, nothing is worse than losing to York Academy. And until the Hall gets its own pool, York will win every swim meet. But that's not going to happen: the Hall's budget is $50,000 short. School pride is plummeting. Boots's father might even transfer him.

But Bruno has a brilliant plan. They'll take matters into their own hands. How hard can it be to raise fifty grand? A few bake sales, a talent show . . . they'll be there in no time, won't they?

Won't they?

ISBN 978-1-4431-2493-5